A Scot's Pledge

The MacLomain Series
End of an Era
Book One

Sky Purington

Story Overview

Accustomed to watching over things for Clan MacLomain and their Viking ancestors, Julie had given up hope of traveling back in time for love like those before her. Until the day an old friend turned crush shows up on her doorstep in New Hampshire claiming he needs help in fourteenth century Scotland.

Having pledged to help his clan, Laird Tiernan MacLomain searches for his destined Broun in the twenty-first century. Yet he only wants the woman he's secretly loved for years. So he breaks the rules and brings Julie back to the medieval period with him. She might lack the bloodline needed to harness the power of the Claddagh, but he won't leave her behind.

Together, they embark on a whirlwind quest to protect King David II against Edward Balliol and his disenfranchised nobles, the 'disinherited.' They also face a dark threat nobody foresaw. Will Tiernan and Julie defeat it without the power of predestined love? Or will breaking the rules be their ultimate downfall and Scotland's ruin? Find out in A Scot's Pledge, an emotional and passionate journey into the turbulent onset of the Second War of Scottish Independence.

COPYRIGHT © 2019
A Scot's Pledge
Sky Purington

This is a work of fiction. Names, characters, places, and incidents
are either the product of the author's imagination or are used
fictitiously, and any resemblance to actual persons living or dead,
business establishments, events, or locales, is entirely coincidental.

Edited by *Cathy McElhaney*
Cover Art by *Tara West*

Published in the United States of America

Dedication

For Scotland's national animal.

Might the *sròin-adharcach* always watch over its beloved country.

Alba gu brath!

Series Overview

'End of an Era' can mean many things, but for the MacLomain Clan, it marked the beginning of the end of their way of life. Only four short years after King Robert the Bruce led Scotland to freedom in the First War of Scottish Independence, the Second War of Scottish Independence began between the Kingdom of Scotland and the Kingdom of England. Though Robert's wee son, David II, was made king, Edward Balliol, with the discreet backing of Edward III of England, challenged him for the throne.

Sworn to protect the rightful king, five Scot's and their lasses go to David's aid defending him against Balliol, and his band of disenfranchised nobles called the 'disinherited.' Though the nobles are mere mortals, the secret brotherhood who control them, are anything but. Worse yet, fighting them will come at a cost to each noble Scot. One destined to change life as they know it. And so the story goes...

Prologue

Parish of Cardross, Scotland
7 June 1329

"IT WILLNAE BE long now," Adlin said softly. He rested his hand against King Robert the Bruce's forehead and tried to lend him peace. "He has but minutes left."

Grant remained silent on the other side of the bed, respecting the imminent passing of a legend. A great man who had done so much for his country. He had known Robert since the king was but a child, so he also mourned the loss of a friend.

Yet as often happened before death came upon folk, Robert stirred.

His eyes fluttered open and his gaze locked on Grant.

"Old friend," he whispered. "Ye are here." His gaze drifted to Adlin. "Both of ye."

"Aye," Grant replied. "We thought it high time for a visit."

Robert's voice was gruff. "Ye mean ye've come to pay yer respects." He noted Grant's ethereal form. "It cannae be any other way with ye sent from the afterlife."

"Och, nay—" Adlin began, but Robert cut him off.

"Whilst I would like to catch up on our many times together," he managed, "I best make these final words count." His gaze went from Adlin to Grant. "Ye'll need to look after my son as ye looked after me."

"But of course," Grant assured. "Ye have our word."

"Things willnae be easy for him," Robert whispered. "The bloody Sassenach will try to take my throne straight away." He was so weak he had trouble shaking his head. "And my wee bairn is but five winters old."

"He will be all right," Adlin said, fully aware Sir Thomas Randolph, 1st Earl of Moray, Guardian of Scotland would see to things. At least for a few years. "Ye need not fear for wee David. Rest, old friend."

Grant nodded in reassurance, lending him peace as well.

Knowing his son had the same guardians watching over him that had watched over Robert most of his life, the Bruce, at last, closed his eyes. Moments later, the death rattle came, and he breathed his last breath.

Though sad for the passing of a noble king and old friend, they knew this was but the beginning of more change in their beloved country. Robert's death and David II's ascension to the throne would launch the beginning of what would be known as the Second War of Scottish Independence.

Their only hope lay in making sure David II traveled the path he was destined to follow. For if he did not, Scotland's future looked bleak indeed. Yet as their beloved king departed the world, they felt something spark from beyond they never could have anticipated.

A darkness with foul intentions.

An evil that would change everything.

It was, as they would soon find out, the beginning of the end of an era.

Chapter One

North Salem, New Hampshire
December 2019

"HERE'S TO FINALLY meeting two new friends." Julie grinned at the women sitting in her festive living room and held up her glass of red wine in a toast. "Three to go."

Holiday music played softly, and snow fell, the perfect backdrop to the crackling fire and sparkling Christmas tree.

Chloe toasted as well. "Here's to that!"

Madison pushed her eyeglasses up her nose and raised her glass. "At last!"

They drank then resumed chatting, getting along as if they had known each other for years rather than only six months. Having been monitoring the online Broun forum launched years ago, Julie knew things must be happening in medieval Scotland when five women of Broun lineage met up within a week of each other. The same thing had occurred before when MacLomain-Broun connections were about to flare across time.

The mystical true-love connections had begun in the eighteenth century in this very house but had since involved women from the twenty-first century. For the MacLomains, it began in Scotland around the early thirteenth century.

Of course, Julie's new Broun friends knew nothing about any of this.

"Too bad the other girls will be delayed." Chloe tucked a wisp of thick reddish-blonde hair behind her ear and peered out the window at the storm. "When is this weather supposed to let up anyway?"

"As if you don't know." Madison rolled her smoky blue eyes and clipped back her shoulder-length black hair. "If there's a scoop, you know about it." She gestured at the storm. "And in these parts, that's news right now."

Chloe winked, her lively amber eyes twinkling. "Just making conversation."

"Plenty of that to be had." Curious, Madison looked Julie's way. "So when are you going to share this big news of yours? We're dying to know."

Since she realized her friends wouldn't be arriving at the same time as planned, she had been debating this. Initially, she'd envisioned sitting down as a group, maybe having a drink or several, then dropping the bomb on them all at once.

"Hey, it turns out our meeting wasn't a coincidence," she'd say.

"It wasn't?" one would respond.

"Nope, in fact, chances are good you're all a bunch of witches." She'd chuckle and act truly impressed. *"Even better? You're destined for Scotsmen from the medieval period who are either wizards or maybe even dragon shifters. How 'bout that? You all have destined true loves. Fated mates! Pretty damn awesome, right?"*

Naturally, they would be shocked at first. But at least they would all be here, going through it together, with Julie available to answer any questions they might have.

Yet they were not all here.

Was it a big deal going through the whole thing twice? Not really. Just a tad much and not as organized as she liked to keep things. After all, she was fairly practiced at dealing with the MacLomain's Viking ancestors and their time traveling mates. She'd done it enough over the years. As to the MacLomain's Brouns? She had zero practice. She did, however, know a few MacLomains. Maybe she should start there?

She thought about how she'd phrase things.

"So years ago I met these medieval Scottish wizards," she'd say. *"Grant and Adlin."*

"Medieval Scottish wizards?" one of her friends would respond in disbelief. *"You're joking, right?"*

4

"Nope, they exist. I've mostly dealt with Adlin lately, though," she would inform, smiling fondly because she couldn't help herself when she thought about his prodigy. *"And his son, Tiernan."*

"You seem fond of Tiernan," would be the reply.

"Definitely." She'd recall the many times she had seen him over the past year and a half. *Time went by differently between Scotland and New Hampshire, so years flew by there where only months passed here. Therefore, she'd known Tiernan his whole life.* "He's such a great person. Always has been."

He was too. At every age. Not only was he kind and thoughtful but powerful.

Not to mention hot.

"*So* damn hot," she murmured.

"Hot?" Madison frowned in confusion before her brows flew up in surprise. "So, this news is about a guy then?"

She blinked, not sure what to say because technically it *was* about a guy. Several of them, for that matter. Not just Tiernan but his cousins if she were to guess. Yet again, she bit back a frown. While the other guys were fine, something about Tiernan being meant for a Broun just didn't sit right. Being meant for any woman actually.

God, she wished her best friend Viv was here to coach her through this, but alas, she fell in love with a Viking dragon and moved to medieval Scandinavia. Somewhere, quite frankly, Julie thought she would be by now too, but evidently not. It seemed she was just the overseer of homes meant to usher in the next round of love connections.

"Well?" Chloe prompted, pulling Julie from her sad, loveless reverie. "Who's the guy then?" The corner of her mouth curled up. "He must be something for you to gather us all together to tell us about him."

"He's...um..." What the hell was she supposed to say? *He's a hottie from the fourteenth century who travels through time fairly often to visit me. I've known him since he was an infant which wasn't all that long ago. Oh, and now I've got a thing for him. How crazy is that?*

No, that wouldn't work.

Madison cocked her head. "He's...um, *what*, Julie?"

Thankfully, someone knocked on the front door before she could respond.

It never occurred to her that nobody should be knocking on the door at this hour, especially in this storm. So she was completely caught off guard when she opened the door to the man she'd just been thinking about.

Her heart leapt into her throat at the sight of him.

"Tiernan," she whispered, unable to find her voice.

He had aged some since she last saw him, and it only made him that much hotter. Tall and broad-shouldered, his dark hair offset his gorgeous pale blue eyes. His face was still a chiseled masterpiece, and his well-sculptured lips just begged to be kissed.

"Julie," he said softly. His warm gaze lingered on her face. "It's been too long."

One month, two days, and eight hours to be precise. "It has."

They continued staring at each other, the moment stretching before her friends snapped them out of it.

"Is this him then?" Chloe eyed him with appreciation as she and Madison joined Julie at the door.

"It must be." Though less obvious, Madison's appreciative gaze was just as thorough. "Aren't you going to invite your boyfriend in out of the cold, Julie?"

"He's not my boyfriend," she managed. It felt like the temperature had spiked a thousand degrees, she was so flustered. "This is my good friend, Tiernan."

Pull yourself together, Julie, she preached. *You can do this.*

Gathering herself, she finally did what she should have done from the start. She invited him in and embraced him like always. Yet it felt awkward this time. Really good but definitely awkward. But why? It had never been this way.

Deep down, she knew, though.

Something had shifted between them. Or maybe something had just become more obvious. What that was, however, was sort of hard to pinpoint. Or was it? Because the way he looked at her was telling.

Tiernan held her a moment longer than she expected before he stepped back and nodded hello to her friends who introduced themselves before she had a chance to. Only then, finally free of her he's-actually-here stupor, did she realize he wasn't dressed in his medieval Scottish garb but twenty-first-century clothing. She took in his jeans, black sweater, and jacket, curious about what he was up to.

"This is for you and your friends, lass," he said to Chloe and handed her a red velvet box. "A gift for the holidays." He handed a smaller box to Julie. "And for you, Jules."

He was the only person beside Viv who called her by that nickname.

"Thank you." She took his jacket. "I didn't know you'd be here." Then she thought better of that statement. His timing couldn't be more perfect considering her friends thought her big news was about a guy. So she added, "With gifts."

"I couldn't help myself." He smiled at Chloe and Madison, his brogue turned way down but still sexy as sin. "It is that time of year, aye?" He turned his heart-stopping smile Julie's way. "I was so looking forward to meeting your friends."

No doubt, he was, and it hurt like hell.

She forced a smile, wondering which one of them he was destined for. In her opinion, the two here weren't quite a fit. While it worked fine for her profession as a journalist and didn't bother Julie any, Chloe was too inquisitive. She'd drive Tiernan nuts with her endless questions. He had a clan to run, so constantly having to answer her would be a no go.

And Madison? She was very nice, but dry on occasion, her obsession with numbers a bit much. Again, good for her job as an accountant, but was that really Tiernan's thing? Sure, he appreciated intelligence, but she couldn't see him talking numbers morning, noon, and night.

"Right. Night," she muttered, again speaking aloud without meaning to. Tiernan and Madison probably wouldn't be talking numbers but doing something else. She frowned at the thought, eyeing Madison with her lithe height. It suited his six foot five frame well, didn't it? Everything would line up just perfectly in bed.

When the three of them looked at Julie in question, wondering what she meant, she improvised though not overly well.

"Night...you know." She gestured out the window. "It's night, so we should..." Think, Jules. Say something halfway intelligent. "Drink." She nodded once. "We should definitely drink."

"Aye, lass, I'm up for a wee dram if you have one." Almost as if he knew what she'd been thinking about, Tiernan's eyes sparkled with amusement. He had to be amused by something else, though. Because his wizardly telepathy could only happen with his kin and his destined love.

"A wee dram it is," Julie said, at last herself with him. Comfortable despite her helpless attraction. But then Tiernan made it so easy. She might not see him as much lately, but outside of Viv, he truly was her best friend. Not that Vivienne knew that or even knew about him.

"I wish we knew you were getting us a gift, Tiernan," Chloe commented, peering at the pretty box as they headed into the kitchen.

She knew Chloe purposefully refrained from mentioning that she hadn't known he existed until he showed up at the door.

"Not your fault, sweetie," Julie said. "You didn't know you'd be meeting him, let alone exchanging gifts." She winked at Tiernan then stood on her tiptoes to get the whisky down from the cabinet. "You're my best-kept secret, Tiernan."

Was he ever. She couldn't talk about him to anyone. On the rare times she saw Vivienne, she refrained because she suspected Viv held out hope Julie might end up in Scandinavia. Still, she could have shared because there's no way she was meant for him. Yet every time she had started to, she'd bitten her tongue. Maybe she just hadn't wanted her friend to remind her of the cold hard truth.

To drive home the fact Julie was in love with a man she could never have.

"Am I then?" Tiernan murmured in her ear, standing so close his front brushed her back when he grabbed the whisky for her. "Yer best-kept secret then, lass?"

She stilled at his closeness, the heat of his body, at the way his brogue thickened, which only happened when his emotions were high. As a rule, MacLomains said 'you' instead of 'ye' so that their twenty-first century counterparts understood them better, but occasionally they slipped.

Her heart leapt when his eyes fell to hers, and he didn't step away.

Where she had sensed sparks between them his last few visits, what simmered between them now was so much more. Sizzling heat flared under her skin, and her breath caught. When his pupils flared, and his gaze fell to her lips, she knew he felt the same.

"Oh, *wow*," Chloe gushed. "These are *beautiful*!"

Though tough, she dragged her eyes away from his face only to see Chloe and Madison admiring the contents of the velvet box. Five gorgeous platinum Claddagh rings were lined up inside, just waiting for their destined Broun.

Despite knowing full well she had no Broun blood and could never be meant for Tiernan, her foolish heart sank. When had she started growing so hopeful? When had she begun praying for a miracle? Because she had and realized it when that box was opened. She'd begun fantasizing that by some amazing twist of fate, there would be six rings in there. That despite possessing no magic or having the correct lineage, she might be destined for him anyway.

But no.

There were only five rings, and all hope was lost.

Until that is, she remembered he had given her a box too.

-A Scot's Pledge-

Chapter Two

HE HAD SWORN he would seek out his destined Broun when he arrived in New Hampshire, but after one look at Julie, he knew it was a lost cause. How could he ever love another? How could anyone but her ever be meant for him?

"They're gorgeous," Julie murmured. Though she stared at the rings, she hadn't moved. Rather, she seemed disinclined to shift away from him. To put any more distance between them.

Lord, she was beautiful. He wanted to finally run his fingers through her curly dark red hair. To lose himself in her thickly lashed deep emerald eyes flecked with pale green. Taste her plush lips at last. He dared not think about what else he wanted to do to her because this was no place to get aroused. Especially when no amount of magic could eliminate an untimely erection.

Not when it came to her.

"You really shouldn't have," Chloe gushed, still admiring the rings. "These had to have cost a fortune."

Only if he let clan and country down because he wanted nothing to do with those rings. Not if Julie wasn't wearing one of them.

Right now, however, they served a purpose.

"Please," he urged Chloe. "Pick out any one you like."

Because the magical rings would find precisely who they were meant for.

Not only that, but they would make Julie's life a lot easier once they were on her friends' fingers.

"You should open yours as well," he said to Julie.

He almost wished he hadn't gotten her anything after he saw the quickly masked disappointment in her eyes at the contents of the other box. Then again, while she might grow more disappointed at the contents of her own box, now he knew with certainty that his feelings for her weren't one-sided.

His father had started bringing him here to visit her when he was very young. Though Julie was but a friendly face then, she became so much more when he was around fifteen. He supposed that made sense considering his age, but it made for far too many excruciating years since then pining for her. Worse still, when he finally caught up with her age-wise, he was not allowed to act on it. Now he was roughly three years older than her and still unable to move beyond their bloody friendship.

Or at least that had been his mindset before arriving.

Now he intended something else entirely despite how very wrong it was.

"It's lovely, Tiernan," Julie whispered, having opened her box. Her eyes were misty, perhaps from both disappointment and being genuinely touched. "Truly."

"You remember then?" he said softly. "What I promised you?"

"Yeah." She offered a wobbly smile and admired the magically blown glass encasing the small thistle flower. "You said you wanted to bring me something from your homeland." She fingered the delicate pendant. "This. A thistle."

He pulled out the dainty chain and pendant then urged her to turn around so he could put it on her. "Do you recall why?"

"Of course." She held her hair out of the way. "Because though the thistle symbolizes many things, graciousness and protection suited me best."

"Aye." He inhaled her soft floral scent. It had been hers for as long as he could remember. "Because you are a gracious protector, Jules," he murmured softly in her ear so her friends couldn't hear him. "One way or another, you have watched over both this house and the Maine chalet for years, and been there when we needed you. Without these two properties, we MacLomains and our Viking ancestors might never have found our destined loves, and so much might have gone wrong." It took everything in him not to kiss her cheek, then turn her lips to his. "The world as we know it might not exist. Certainly not Scotland."

12

"I think you're giving me a bit too much credit." Julie admired the pendant as he secured the clasp. "But it's lovely all the same." She met his eyes over her shoulder. "Really. I love it. Thank you, Tiernan."

Even the sound of her saying his name affected him. He wanted to pull her into his arms. To finally kiss her once and for all. How could he care so much for a woman God didn't want him to be with? Surely, magic was askew this time because the good Lord *must* want this for them.

"It's a perfect fit," Chloe declared, admiring her ring. "And..."

"What is it?" Madison asked, sliding her own ring on as well.

Just like Chloe, a strange look came over her face.

Julie glanced from woman to woman and frowned. "Are you guys all right?"

"Yeah," Chloe whispered. "I just had the strangest feeling come over me."

"Me too," Madison murmured. "Like warmth and anticipation..."

When she trailed off, Chloe continued. "Like something amazing is about to happen." Her eyes narrowed a fraction. "Something a little scary too."

"Right." Madison yawned. "Wow, I'm suddenly super wiped."

Chloe yawned as well. "I second that."

Julie glanced from Tiernan to them, evidently understanding magic was at work because she went with it. "Why don't we skip drinks and crash early?"

"You don't mind?" Chloe's eyes were already drifting. "We haven't even eaten the lasagna you made for us yet."

"You mean bought." Julie chuckled. "I make a killer drink, but cooking isn't my strong point." She ushered them upstairs. "C'mon, off to bed with you. We'll chat more over coffee in the morning."

"Are you sure?" Madison asked on another yawn, offering Tiernan a little wave goodbye.

"Positive," Julie replied before the three of them vanished upstairs.

He downed a shot of whisky, poured another, refilled Julie's glass, and strolled through a house that had now seen five generations of MacLomains come and go. As to his own direct line, four generations. It was hard to believe his great-grandfather Iain had stood in this very foyer. That he had been in this living room with Tiernan's great-grandmother Arianna, who had lived here in the eighteenth century.

He admired Julie's Christmas tree, sad that she had spent so many holidays alone, caught in limbo as she was. Or that was how he had always seen it. She had inadvertently helped bring several couples together, but what about her? Who was she meant for?

Him if he had any say in it.

Which, as it happened, he now did because of his intentions to go rogue and break all the rules. He stoked the fire with a flick of his wrist and noted the picture of her and Sean on the mantle.

"He was a good friend," Julie said softly, back downstairs in record time. She joined him in front of the fire and set the bottle of whisky on the mantle. "The last time I saw Viv, she said he and Svala were doing well in tenth-century Scandinavia."

In truth, Julie had been interested in Sean at one time, but it wasn't meant to be. Which again made Tiernan wonder at her role in all this beyond the obvious. He'd always suspected she must be destined for someone. It seemed too unfair otherwise. His father Adlin and now deceased great uncle Grant surely would have had someone in mind for her. She deserved love like all the rest. More so, in his opinion.

He handed Julie her wine. "Are your friends off to sleep then?"

"They are." Her knowing eyes met his. "So, what was that all about? What did you do to their rings?" She cocked her head. "And where'd you get them from? Your dad?"

"Naturally," he replied. "With a touch of Grant in there too, I'm sure."

"Right, from the afterlife." She shook her head and chuckled. "Sometimes, I forget just how crazy things can get with you MacLomains." She sipped her wine. "So my friends are what, cast under some sort of spell?"

"You could say that," he replied. "The rings will take whoever wears them on their own journey and help them to understand all of this. Make them believe and accept their circumstances easier than they might have otherwise."

"Ah," she murmured, understanding. "So basically, I won't need to explain what's going on and what lies ahead."

"If the rings work as they should," he said, "your friends should find their way along just fine."

14

"*If* they work as they should?" She narrowed her eyes, knowing him far too well. "What's going on, Tiernan? While I love seeing you, why are you here? What's happening in Scotland?"

"We're still trying to figure that out." He downed his whisky and set his cup on the mantle. "My magic started fluctuating when I was helping my Viking ancestors. When I returned to Scotland, I discovered that magic was fluctuating in all corners of my country."

"I'm so sorry." Worry drew her finely arched eyebrows together. "Any idea why?"

"Nay," he said. "All we know is the source of the disturbance originated around the year thirteen twenty-nine. Specifically, when King Robert the Bruce's five-year-old son David II ascended to the throne upon his father's death."

"Though tempted to say that's awfully specific, I know what you and your father are capable of." She poured him more whisky. "And, yet again, Grant from the afterlife."

"What I *was* capable of," he corrected and sighed. "I barely came through for my Viking ancestors, and I fear it's only going to get worse." He shook his head, troubled, more open with her than anyone about his true feelings. When he was at home, being chieftain, he had to remain strong, but here with her, he could let his guard down and finally share his concerns. His true feelings. "My magic waning feels like a piece of my soul is being ripped out, Jules. I feel…weak…helpless."

"But you're not." She handed him his glass, urged him to drink, and said everything he needed to hear. "You're a seasoned warrior with a good head on your shoulders. Always remember that, Tiernan. You're far more than an arch-wizard. You're kind, a good friend, a protector, and a damn good leader."

"You're prejudiced." He nearly brushed a tempting curl back from the corner of her eye but refrained. "But thank you."

"I might be prejudiced," she conceded. "But I'm also right." Then, because she wasn't one to let him dwell in misery any longer than he would her, she remained focused on the facts. "So little David becomes king, and somehow that ignites something that affects magic in Scotland in your day and age, thirteen forty-six, roughly seventeen years later, right?"

He nodded. "Precisely."

"Thoughts?"

"The only thing of consequence that has happened recently in my era is King David losing to the British at Nevillie's Cross near Durham." He shrugged. "The consequence of that is him being taken captive for eleven winters."

"Then what?"

"Then, under the Treaty of Berwick, a ransom of one hundred thousand merks will be agreed upon, and he returns to Scotland to continue ruling."

"How long will he rule for?"

"Nigh on forty-two winters."

She sipped her wine and thought about that. "What would've happened had he not ruled that long?"

"'Tis hard to know." He shrugged. "Edward Balliol might have become king, or mayhap another would have risen up against him." He shook his head. "Having known us MacLomains and our Viking Sigdir ancestors this long, you know there are too many possibilities to count when it comes to historical outcomes."

"Very true," she murmured, still thinking it over. "So chances are pretty good that whatever went wrong happened between David becoming king in thirteen twenty-nine and your era, thirteen forty-six."

"What makes you say that?" He eyed her curiously. "It could just as easily be something that happened after thirteen forty-six."

"I don't know," she said softly. "Just a feeling." She eyed him. "You agree, though, don't you?"

How curious for her to have such a specific feeling. One more aligned with his thoughts than seemed entirely natural. Could there be something to that? Or was he just grasping for anything right now?

"Aye, I do agree," he said. "Though 'tis always a possibility, I dinnae think anything that happened after he's captured in my era has to do with this."

She nodded before she cocked her head and focused on what else he had said. "Who's Edward Balliol?"

"The son of a former Scottish king and a traitor to his country in the first war," he revealed. "He felt he had more claim to the throne than David." He shook his head. "From what I've heard, he's a bloody bastard. Once David was declared king, Balliol rallied the disinherited to his cause and—"

16

"The disinherited?" Her brows snapped together, and she frowned. "Who are they?"

Caught by the strange look in her eyes, he explained.

"Bloody traitors just like Balliol," he muttered. "They were Scottish nobles who supported England rather than the Bruce during the First War of Scottish Independence. When the war ended, and The Treaty of Edinburgh-Northampton was signed, King Robert didnae allow them to keep their land. So 'twas no surprise they didnae want the Bruce's heir to be king."

He downed his whisky and went on.

"One of those "disinherited" was Edward Balliol himself," he explained. "With the discreet backing of Edward III of England, Balliol demanded the return of his ancestral lands. When he didnae get what he wanted, he invaded Scotland." He bit back a sneer. "Then the bloody arse had himself crowned King of Scots, despite wee David II, the rightful king, already holding the title."

He could see her mental wheels spinning when he finished.

"What is it, Julie?" he said. "What was that look I saw in your eyes at the mention of the disinherited?"

"I had a look?"

"Aye, you had a look."

"Just…" She clearly struggled for the right words. "They're at the root of it, Tiernan." She shook her head. "I know it like I know nothing else."

Though tempted to question her, he saw a plausible reason, better yet, an eventual explanation for what he had intended to do since the moment he laid eyes on her. Was he risking everything? Aye. Did he care? Naturally.

But he was going to do it anyway and said so.

"Then you will be needed," he said firmly, trying to sound like he spoke with logic rather than emotion. She might not possess magic, but she was clearly on to something here. Certain knowledge that might blossom into even more knowledge as time went by. "You will come home with me this time Julie."

17

-A Scot's Pledge-

Chapter Three

"NO," SHE REPLIED automatically to Tiernan's declaration that she return home with him. She ignored the way her heart leapt with hope. The excitement his words invoked. It was her role to hold down the fort here, not travel back in time. Not embark on a grand adventure and fall in love.

Why was that, though?

Because you're not a Broun, she reminded herself. *You're not meant to find an unbelievable connection across time.*

But why?

Because you're not a witch or dragon, that's why. You're just a mere mortal.

"You're so much more than that, Julie," Tiernan said softly.

"Why?" she whispered, convinced he really was hearing her thoughts.

"Why do I think you're more than just a mere mortal?"

"No." She shook her head and found her tongue. "You can hear my thoughts, can't you?" She narrowed her eyes, still far too hopeful. "Why is that when you never could before?"

It must be a glitch in the system.

A bizarre side effect of his magic fluctuating.

"I dinnae know." He clenched his fist for about the fifth time since they were standing there.

"And why do you keep doing that?" She gestured at his clenched fist and frowned. "I've seen you pent up before, but you never did that." She searched his eyes. "What the hell's going on, Tiernan?

19

Truth time. Why are you saying I should travel back in time with you when we both know that's impossible? I won't be needed for anything because I'm not a Broun, and I have no magic."

Something he evidently didn't care all that much about based on the way he looked at her. She ignored her pounding heart, planted her fists on her hips, and eyed him curiously. He wasn't being straight with her. Yet should she really push this? Should she essentially drive him away from her? Because if she reacted off the building desire in his unwavering gaze, that's precisely what she would be doing.

"If you didn't feel Chloe or Madison might be your true love," she said matter-of-factly, "then you've got to wait for the other three." She widened her eyes at him and emphasized her point. "*Five* women, *five* Claddagh rings." She shook her head. "*Not* six."

He went to speak, then stopped, clearly searching for the right words.

"What is it?" she whispered because her damn voice wasn't working right again. The way he looked at her gave her hope she wasn't allowed. Hope she needed to stomp out whether it was real or not. *Push him away now or else. Stand your ground.* But no, she stood there waiting with bated breath wondering what his response would be.

It turned out to be so much more than she anticipated.

"I dinnae want them, Julie," he said so softly she barely caught it. He cleared his throat and spoke louder. "I dinnae want the lasses here, and I willnae want the ones coming."

"I don't understand," she murmured, though she did.

Now her poor heart was downright somersaulting.

He clenched his jaw, still struggling with how to phrase things. How to tell her how he felt. When he finally found his tongue, he didn't say what her traitorous heart hoped to hear but targeted her sense of practicality instead.

"You sensing the disinherited were at the root of this is new," he revealed, dancing around the subject. The real reason he wanted her along. "That you sense such when even powerful wizards dinnae is telling. Important." He shook his head. "'Twould be foolish of me to leave you behind."

I agree she wanted to blurt. *I should be wherever you are.*

Obviously, she didn't voice that, though.

"Why?" While everything inside her wanted to go, she knew better. "Just because I had a feeling the disinherited were at the heart of this doesn't mean I'm needed in Scotland." She gestured at the velvet box he'd set on the mantle. "If Chloe and Madison aren't a fit, then you need to wait for Alyssa, Ciara, and Destiny to arrive because one of them is meant for you." She shook her head, forcing the words out of her mouth. "And how do you know you don't want them when you haven't even met them?"

"Because I want you," he said far more bluntly than she anticipated, apparently bypassing logic now. "I have always wanted you."

It became difficult to think. Breathe. How many times had she fantasized about him saying those words? Hoped against hoped? Too many times to count. But that didn't change anything. Tiernan had a mission, an obligation to his clan and country. Which meant she did too if he thought he could be with her...love her.

She needed to keep his eye on the ball. On what was possible. Real.

"You don't want me," she forced out. While tempted to look anywhere but at him, she kept her gaze steady on him, so he knew she meant business. No wussing out here. "You've known me your whole life, Tiernan. I'm a good friend and confidant." She shook her head. "Nothing more."

"You have been something more for a long time." Evidently, now that he had pushed past the awkwardness, he didn't intend to hold back. "More than a friend. More than a confidant."

"Call it a crush then." She opened the box and showed him the remaining rings. "These are the real thing, Tiernan. True love." She arched a brow and laid it on the line. "How can you contemplate abandoning that for even a second? What about your clan and country? All the people you're responsible for?" She gestured between them. "Because you and I hooking up means you'll never harness the power of the Claddagh ring, and everything'll go to shit." She tilted her head in question. "Is that what you want?"

"You know it's not," he said. "But that doesnae stop the way I feel."

"Like I said, a crush." She shook her head. "Not love."

"Besides," she went on, not giving him a chance to respond. She threw everything out there before she threw her arms around him and declared she'd go to the moon and back with him. "I don't feel the same way." She shrugged, sipped her wine, and at last, looked away, figuring it was time to appear uninterested. "So there you have it. No hope here."

When Tiernan crossed his arms over his chest and let silence settle, seemingly of the mind she was right, Julie bit back disappointment. She'd always had a knack at convincing people to see things her way, which she *should* be happy about right now. This was a *good* thing. She ought to pat herself on the back for being a rock star with words and hiding her true feelings so well.

"Whilst I appreciate your devotion to my country," he finally said, amused rather than resolute and sad like he should be, "your tone gave you away, Jules."

Aww, hell. What tone? "I didn't have a tone."

"You had a tone," he assured.

"Maybe a stern tone." She frowned at him. "One meant to remind you of everything that's at stake right now." She did her best to look disappointed. "Honestly, I'm surprised by this, Tiernan. It's your duty, your responsibility, to put your people first. Before your own wants." She widened her eyes, probably overdoing it at this point, but hell, the amusement on his face was only growing. "If all that isn't enough, I held you when you were a baby! Saw you as a toddler, little boy, pre-teen." She scrunched her nose. "So really, you crushin' on me is just creepy."

"I dinnae know," he mused. "Looking at it that way, I'd say *you* crushing on me is even creepier."

Damn, he had her figured out. But of course, he did. He was a wizard...and her best friend. "How did you get that out of everything I just said?"

"Actually, I've sensed it for quite some time now." He remained perfectly blunt. "When you opened the door tonight, I knew you felt just as strongly as me."

"You don't know that."

"But I do."

"How?"

"Your heart for starters." His eyes twinkled. "'Twas about pounding out of your chest."

"Maybe I'd been dancing..." yeah, right, *so* weak, "with my friends."

The corner of his mouth shot up. "To Christmas music?"

"It can be upbeat."

"You hate dancing."

"I hate sucking at dancing."

"You dinnae suck at dancing."

"Oh, but I do."

"You just havenae had the right partner."

"We're talking about upbeat dancing," she reminded.

"Nay, we're talking about you trying to do what you think is the right thing," he replied. "Pushing me away when all you really want to do is find out what it would be like…at last."

He was *way* too on to her. Yet what precisely was he referring to? It sounded like they might be off the topic of dancing and on to something else. "Being cryptic like your father again, I see."

"You know what I'm talking about."

Definitely not dancing. Right?

"No clue." But she could imagine so very, very well.

"You want to know what it would feel like to dance with me." His tone dropped to a sexy octave that about curled her toes. "Then, mayhap more."

"Definitely not interested in dancing," she lied then grabbed at anything she could. "Okay, I'm just gonna give it to you straight." She thought fast and came up with the perfect argument. "I think your magic going all wonky has you struggling for normalcy, something dependable, and that's always been me. So you're latching on to what makes you feel like you still have control over things."

"Latching on?" he murmured, his gaze all smoldering-bedroom-eyes now. "Good idea." His magic wasn't so wonky that he couldn't flick a wrist and turn the music up. Before she darted away, he reeled her close. "You're right. Latching on to you does make me feel better." His eyes met hers. "In control, as you say."

This was *so* not a good idea. *Stay strong. Step away. Think of Scotland. All the lives depending on him. You're his voice of reason.* Yet, just like it had when he embraced her earlier, all logic fled the moment she was in his arms. Her inner self-coach threw in the towel at the feel of his hard body. At the look in his gorgeous eyes.

She was in way over her head.

Scratch that. She'd already drowned.

"You are not entirely right, though, Jules," he murmured, tilting her chin until her eyes didn't stray from his. As if they ever would. "This doesnae feel normal in the least."

Had she mentioned normal at some point? Because she agreed, this felt anything but. She felt electrified, on fire, like the room—no, the whole house—was fading away. All that existed was him. His hot as hell face, his eyes, lips, the tiny braids that had appeared in his hair…

"Oh, *shit*," she exclaimed, realizing too late he'd pulled her right into his web.

The room *was* really gone.

So was the house.

In fact, her surroundings had changed altogether.

Chapter Four

Monastery of Scone, Scotland
24 November 1331

BEFORE JULIE HAD a chance to say another word, he pulled her into a darkened corner of the stone hallway and put a finger to her lips.

"Shh," he whispered in her ear, standing closer than necessary. "Dinnae say a word until I've had time to assess our surroundings."

Her eyes narrowed, but she remained silent as he looked around. Thankfully, they had arrived where and when he hoped they would but decided she didn't need to know that quite yet. Rather, he preferred to keep her waiting sandwiched between him and the abbey wall. If he had been smart, he would have already kissed her.

After all, he was down the rabbit hole now, wasn't he?

He had always done for his clan and kin, putting them first. Now, with his fool heart at the helm, all he could do was keep Julie with him. Leaving her behind yet again simply wasn't an option. While he knew it was wrong, damning actually, he prayed there was a reason for it. For all the times his father had brought him to visit her. For this pressing need he felt to be around her.

Now he was starting to hear her thoughts. Surely there was something to that.

"You're not looking around anymore," she hissed on a whisper, placing a hand against his chest. She had done it to push him away, yet she didn't. Instead, her hand lingered there, almost as if she couldn't help herself. Genuine worry lit her eyes as they searched his.

"What have you done, Tiernan?" She shook her head. "You need to take me back. I don't belong here."

"Yet, you're here." He fingered her soft curl and murmured a chant that dressed her appropriately. "You finally get your adventure through time, Jules."

"But it's not *my* adventure." She eyed her dark green medieval dress, awed despite herself. "It's someone else's."

"Not with me, it's not." He held out the crook of his elbow. "Now 'tis time to join me and act the proper wife, aye?"

"Wife?" she mouthed and rolled her eyes. Yet he spied the flicker of excitement she tried to hide as she slipped her arm through his. "You're really pushing it."

"'Tis the easiest disguise," he explained, then really did push it just to see. "Would you not want to be my wife then?"

"Hell," she exclaimed, turning wide eyes on him. "You're on a roll, aren't you?"

"You didnae answer my question."

"Because it's a moot point," she whispered out of the corner of her mouth, her cheeks flushed as they made their way into the crowd. He could tell she was trying not to stare at everyone in their fourteenth-century finery.

Curious, he finally tried what he'd been putting off because, quite frankly, he would have been beyond disappointed had it not worked.

"Best that you remain silent now," he said into her mind. *"Your words and accent are foreign."*

She stopped short and stared at him, wide-eyed. "Did you just—"

"Aye," he said telepathically, far more relieved than he let on that she could hear him. This surely proved she was meant for him. Better still, though, would be him hearing her voice too. Not just catching her thoughts. *"'Tis me, Julie. If you but think a response, I should hear you."*

He's out of his mind, she thought. *This is crazy. Impossible. I shouldn't hear him...should I? I'm not a Broun. But heck, he sounds so damn good. Focus, Julie. You're spinning out of control. But then look at these people. Better yet, look at him in his MacLomain plaid lookin' delicious enough to eat.*

"That's thinking to yourself, lass." He couldn't help a small grin. *"Talk directly to me without moving your mouth."*

"Aww, hell," she muttered, blushing, no doubt because of what she'd been thinking.

Please let this work, he thought. *God above, please let him hear her bonny voice in his mind at last.*

"You heard all I was thinking then?" she said into his mind this time. She cleared her throat even though she wasn't using her vocal cords. *"About that last part..."*

He almost yanked her into his arms then, and there, he was so relieved and happy to finally hear her telepathically. He was also more than a bit aroused, so he stopped next to a tree and positioned her in front of him to watch the ceremony.

"I heard everything, lass," he confirmed telepathically. He leaned down as though whispering in her ear for no other reason than to enjoy the scent of her sweet hair. To feel its silky texture against his cheek. *"And I verra much liked that last part. You sound damn good too...and you look just as delicious in that dress...in anything, actually."*

Her breath caught, and she shivered with awareness.

When he rested his hands on her shoulders and stepped even closer, she tensed.

"What are you doing?" she said, her internal voice breathless if that were possible.

"Watching the coronation with you." He pointed at the children in their regal clothes. The boy had thick dark hair like his father and large, soulful eyes. The girl was fairer with light brown locks. *"See the wee lad and lassie over there?"*

"Yes."

"Though parliament appointed him king upon Robert the Bruce's death in thirteen twenty-nine, that is wee seven-year-old King David II about to be crowned," he divulged. *"The ten-year-old next to him is his wee wife, Queen Joan of England."*

"Oh, wow," Julie whispered aloud before she remembered to speak telepathically. *"I can't believe I'm looking at Robert the Bruce's son. That I'm looking at any of this."* She sighed and glanced over her shoulder at him. *"While I'm thankful for the opportunity, I dread the consequences of your actions, Tiernan."* She looked forward again. *"Adlin's gonna be super pissed. Grant, too, I imagine."*

"Not at you." Never at her. His father and Grant had always adored Julie. *"I will deal with da when the time comes."*

"If the time ever comes," she remarked, saying what she thought was right despite her own feelings. *"I know how big a kink in the system you just created with this stunt. You not bringing your Broun along, falling in love, and igniting the power of the Claddagh ring could mean Scotland's ruin and the death of everyone you love."*

"Nay." His heart told him it would be otherwise. That he was on the right track. *Had* to be.

Because he was irrevocably in love with Julie, and nothing would change that.

Forcing himself to love another would be impossible. Not only could love not be forced, but if it somehow could be, such false emotion was not the sort of thing that ignited the Claddagh ring. Love had to be true. Genuine. From the very heart, the very soul. *"I willnae let my country down, lass. You have my word."*

"Well, then you best whisk me back to the future ASAP." She tossed him another look over her shoulder. *"Which could already be days in the future."*

"I dinnae think we need to worry about that."

"Of course we do!"

"Mayhap not." He had been sensing something since they arrived. A familiar magic he never anticipated working quite like this. Or should he say working for him and likely his kin? *"I think my Viking ancestors, or rather their blade, is extending magic that was only supposed to apply to them and their ash trees."*

"What are you talking about?" She kept her eyes on the children being crowned, as curious about that as she was about what he was sharing. *"What trees?"*

He told her about the new magic his Viking ancestors had been given. Magic that allowed them to travel from era to era without losing large amounts of time. It was only supposed to apply to the ashes connecting the past with the future, but he felt the same magic in the sword he now carried.

A blade that was supposed to help him save Scotland.

"Holy crap," she whispered. Her eyes swept over the impressive sword sheathed at his waist before she met his eyes again. *"Are you serious? No more of you aging while I stay the same age?"*

"Aye, that's the premise for my ancestors and their modern-day mates," he replied. *"I sense that magic is lending us the same courtesy."*

"What if your magic's off, though, and you're wrong?" She frowned. *"What if time's still going by much faster here than in the twenty-first century?"*

"It doesnae go by so fast that a few days are going to make a difference," he reminded. *"Until then, my gut and my heart are telling me you are the lass meant to take this journey with me, Jules. Your role of protecting Scotland is not merely looking over properties in the future."*

Their eyes lingered on each other before she turned her attention to the wee bairns again.

"You're playing an awful risky game based on nothing but emotions," she murmured. *"That's seriously not like you."*

It took him a moment to catch her meaning.

"You think my magic is not just faltering but actually affecting my judgment." In truth, she might be right. But then she might be wrong, and he said as much. He finally said what he felt. Something he should have said years ago. Because he was convinced this could work despite her not having Broun lineage. *"Magic might be capable of many things, but it doesnae control love nor manifest it. 'Tis the other way around. Love ignites magic...and I love you."*

She went perfectly still and offered no reply right away.

Unfortunately, when she did, it wasn't precisely the response he was hoping for. But then he should have known she would put him and his country first. Which essentially is what she was doing when she tried to push him away.

"We do love each other, Tiernan...as friends." Her eyes met his again. *"Always as friends."* She rubbed her lips together as though ready to speak aloud but looked back at the children and continued telepathically. *"I think you might be confusing things. Sure, our love is real and granted we're attracted to each other, but that doesn't mean we're head over heels."* She shook her head, lying through her telepathic teeth. *"It just doesn't."*

But it did, and they both knew it.

"Somehow, whatever's going on in this era is turning everything around on you." She sighed. *"Point blank, you're letting your emotions rule you when you should be focused on your duty as*

chieftain. On protecting your country. And I'm gonna make sure you remember that at every opportunity."

Yet she subconsciously leaned back against him as the coronation came to an end. While she claimed one thing, her body and thoughts said another. She tremored when he ran his hands slowly from her shoulders down her arms, and her turbulent thoughts revealed the truth.

She wanted this to be real but feared it wasn't.

"Come," he finally said aloud and offered her his elbow again. "'Tis time to introduce ourselves."

Surprise lit her eyes. "Introduce ourselves?"

"Aye." He grinned. "After all, we are here to protect wee David as was promised his father on his deathbed."

Chapter Five

AS IT TURNED out, they did not get a chance to meet King David for a few more hours. By the time they did, Joan of England had already departed, off to her family's holding. David, she soon discovered, was quiet and withdrawn, staring at her more than he spoke. If anything, they dealt more with Sir Thomas Randolph, 1st Earl of Moray, who had been appointed Guardian of Scotland.

A man, as it happened, who knew Adlin.

Thomas was Robert the Bruce's nephew and had been a military commander in many battles during the First War of Scottish Independence. Battles that Adlin and his cousins had ensured went as they should back when they came together with their Brouns. Because Thomas was Robert the Bruce's trusted confidant, he knew about the MacLomains. More so, of what they were capable.

Why they were there then and why they might be here now.

Somewhere in his fifties with grayish light brown hair, Thomas was a distinguished, weathered man who had clearly seen his fair share of war. Yet he had the distinct air of a diplomat as he urged them to sit across from him, and introductions were made. Meanwhile, David left, evidently not needing to sit in on this.

As they continued speaking with Thomas, she realized she no longer needed to pretend to be Tiernan's wife. Not that it had been such a difficult chore. Still, best not to continue playing the role. Especially when it felt so natural. So meant to be when it wasn't. Something she better keep in mind.

"Ye look a great deal like yer da, lad." Thomas eyed Tiernan. "It has been many years. How is Adlin?"

"Well." Tiernan grinned. "Enjoying retirement with ma."

"Ah, Milly. One doesnae forget a lass like her nor the lasses who came after her." Thomas's appreciative gaze slid to Julie. "Are ye from foreign lands like them, then? A match for Tiernan?"

"Yes, I'm from a foreign land," she confirmed, finally speaking aloud. "But I'm not meant for Tiernan. We're just friends."

"Foreign ye say?" He scratched his temple. "But ye sound like ye're from here."

Julie and Tiernan glanced at each other, confused.

"Ye dinnae hear her accent?" Tiernan asked. "Truly?"

"Nay, she doesnae sound like the others I met all those years ago if that's what ye're getting at." Thomas narrowed his eyes. "Ye mean to say she isnae from these parts?"

"Nay," Tiernan said softly, clearly perplexed. "But that's neither here nor there."

Thomas crossed his arms over his chest and sighed. "Trouble's afoot again, aye?" He muttered a curse about a pretender being nothing but King Edward's puppet. "More than that bloody weakling Balliol pretending he has a claim to the throne?"

"Aye, so it seems," Tiernan confirmed. "We dinnae know precisely what the trouble is yet, though. Only that 'tis important we keep a close eye on wee David. Not only because 'twas Robert the Bruce's wishes but because of this unknown threat. If for some reason, we cannae, ye need to be vigilant and keep more guards around him than usual."

Thomas nodded, understanding how dire it was if Tiernan were here. "So ye've no clue where this threat comes from? What I should be prepared for?"

"Not yet." Tiernan glanced from Julie to Thomas, evidently taking her suggestion about the disinherited quite seriously. "But 'twould be prudent to keep an eye out for the men Balliol is rallying to his cause. Traitorous nobles who felt deprived of Scottish land in the last war."

"Och, bloody traitors dinnae deserve to even call themselves Scotsmen," Thomas spat. His bushy brows furrowed in wariness. "But at least they are blood and flesh men we can fight." His gaze narrowed on Tiernan. "'Twas my understanding that yer da and kin fought something a wee bit different."

"They did and still do," Tiernan confirmed. "Pure evil."

"Ye think the nobles are part of this evil then?"

"We dinnae know quite yet," Tiernan replied. "But we soon will. Dinnae doubt it." His gaze remained steady on Thomas, his words firm. "We will get to the root of this and help ye and yer men keep King David safe."

Thomas considered him for a moment before he nodded once. "I believe ye mean that." His attention returned to Julie. "And yer role in this, lass? Because 'tis clear ye've a part." His brow inched up in amused astuteness. "As it were, I dinnae recall the lasses who joined Adlin and his kin being mere friends. Each and every one was quite enamored with their MacLomain." He mulled that over. "Or, if I recall correctly, those with MacLomain bloodlines. Hamilton's and MacLeod's, as well, I believe."

He clearly had a very good memory.

"Tiernan has always been a good friend." She wasn't about to admit to anything else. "I try to be there for my friends."

In retrospect, that sounded sort of silly, but what the hell else was she supposed to say? Because she certainly wasn't going to tell him that Tiernan had risked everything by bringing her here. That he was out of his mind for doing this.

Never mind the astounding experience of finally traveling back in time, she was still trying to get over him saying he loved her. Just like that, in the middle of a medieval coronation of all things, he just dropped that bomb. She swore her whole world exploded in joy before reality, yet again came crashing down.

Then there was the whole talking telepathically thing.

She'd always thought that was a cool perk for those who had fallen in love over the years but had no idea how *amazing* it actually was. It felt like mixing Tiernan's toe-curling sexpot voice with a kick-ass, shoot you to oblivion orgasm. Which made her wonder, how the hell did those couples save the world talking telepathically? She would've been on her back with her legs spread the whole time.

"You bloody well better stop thinking like that," Tiernan warned, yet there was amusement in his internal voice. *"Or we're doomed before we've begun, lass."*

"Get out of my head already," she shot back, forgetting he could hear her thoughts. *"You weren't supposed to catch that."*

"Sorry." He didn't sound sorry in the least, though. *"I cannae control what I hear."*

"Somehow, I doubt that."

"I see," Thomas said to her, responding to her comment about her and Tiernan being friends. "Well, then, I thank ye for coming to the aid of yer friend."

The way he said 'friend' told her he was no fool.

"Will ye need lodging?" Thomas asked. "We'll be staying here for the eve, then heading back to David's residence on the morn."

"I didnae see many soldiers about," Tiernan commented, likely aware of the location of Thomas's every warrior, whether visible or not. "Have ye enough for a traveling guard?"

"Aye, most are out of sight right now," Thomas assured. "'Twas best for the ceremony."

Tiernan nodded. "'Tis our hope to join ye. Lodging would be appreciated."

"Aye then, I'll show ye the way."

She smiled when she spied David peeking around the corner, then vanish as they headed down the hallway. He might be withdrawn, but he was curious.

As it turned out, they were given a cottage with a single small bed, which meant they had to sleep together. *Wonderful.* How was she supposed to stick to her guns when she was lying in bed with him? One that provided no wiggle room? She eyed the earthen floor already knowing she wouldn't ask Tiernan to sleep on it even though he would. While she might try lying on it herself, he'd never allow it.

"'Tis this or a tent," Thomas had said. "Plenty of that on the morrow."

"'Tis fine," Tiernan had assured before Thomas left, having let them know he'd send someone with food and drink. A cool wind blew in through the rafters, and pine needles rained down outside the window. It was pretty here, reminding her a lot of New Hampshire's woodland.

"This is working out a little too perfectly for you, isn't it?" she remarked.

"You know I'll sleep on the floor."

"And you know I won't let you."

He set aside the Viking sword, and sank down on the bed, his expression on her but not really seeing her.

"What is it?" She sat beside him, wondering when she would start catching his thoughts or if it was a one-way street.

"'Tis curious is all," he murmured, clearly off the conundrum of their sleeping arrangements. "Not just us being able to speak telepathically but that Thomas didnae hear your true accent."

"That *was* weird," she agreed. "Has that ever happened before in all the generations of modern day time travelers?"

"Not that I know of," he said. "We need to talk to da. See what he makes of it."

"Okay." She stood and motioned that he get moving along. "Chant me home then back to MacLomain Castle you go."

"There's no time." He stood as well. "First to the castle, then we will see."

"We will not see!" She planted her fists on her hips and cocked her head at him. "Enough is enough, Tiernan. We can't keep doing this."

"This?"

"Yes, *this*." She gestured at the cottage and bed, knowing she could only be so strong. "I shouldn't be part of looking after David with you, and I sure as heck shouldn't be in this little cottage spending the night with you."

Back to himself, the corner of his mouth curled up, and a twinkle lit his eyes. "Why not?"

"You know full well why not."

"Are you telling me you cannae manage a night in bed with me?"

"Not a bed that size."

He glanced from the bed to her, his amusement only growing. "There's room enough to sleep."

"Yeah, spooning and heck if you don't know it."

"What's the matter with spooning?"

She tried not to, she really did, but her gaze dropped to his groin, and she pointed out his very obvious, not to mention damn impressive, erection. "I think we both know the answer to that."

"There's no helping it, lass." He chuckled, and his brogue thickened. "Not when ye get that look in yer eyes every time ye glance at the bed."

"What look?"

"The same one ye had at the door in New Hampshire, then when we danced, then—"

"Then nothing," she cut him off. "Because I don't have a look."

"You do." He stepped far too close and brushed his thumb along her cheek. "'Tis a becoming pink here with a wee bit o' drift to your eyes as if you might be envisioning me minus my—"

"Minus your nothing," she interrupted. "I mean *something*." She was all turned around at the look in his eyes, the way his weapon-roughened thumb felt against her skin. "I...we..." She nearly leaned her cheek into his touch but caught herself and pulled away. "Just chant away your erection, then chant me home."

"Do you consider the colonial your home?" he murmured, surprising her with the question.

"For now," she replied. "Until I end up at the Maine chalet again waiting for the next round of time travelers meant for hot Vikings."

He frowned. "Hot?"

Ah, perhaps *this* was the way to drive him into a Broun's arms.

"Yeah, smokin' hot Vikings, actually." But not as hot as him. Nobody was as hot as Tiernan. Not in her book. Best to keep on with the charade, though. So she pretended to ponder. "Honestly, I figured I'd end up with a Viking dragon shifter...was kinda hoping I—"

That's all she got out before he yanked her against him, and any foolish pretend notion she might have had about Vikings flew right out the window.

Chapter Six

THOUGH HE KNEW full well Julie was interested in him, and only him, something about her speculating about a Viking brought out a possessive streak he had no idea he possessed. One he was bloody glad for when he finally did what he had wanted to do for years.

He kissed her.

The moment their lips touched, he knew he was right. She might not be a Broun, but she was his. She always had been and always would be.

He cupped the back of her neck and kept the kiss gentle and exploratory at first, pleased when she didn't try to pull away but melted against him. How many times had he imagined this moment? How sweet she would taste? How receptive she would be? He never once envisioned her being otherwise. Never once pulling away or not wanting this as much as him.

It would be too crushing. Too final.

Lost in the way her mouth felt against his, how her body trembled when he deepened the exchange, he vaguely wondered why his magic hadn't ignited. Because he had intended to distract her with a kiss and whisk her back to his castle. Something she must have suspected because it snapped her out of the sensual place they were in.

"Oh, no," she groaned, tearing her lips away. She wiggled out of his arms. "Damn it all, Tiernan, why'd you do that!"

He sighed and raked a hand through his hair. "Honestly?"

"No," she said, trying for sarcasm, but sounding more breathless than anything. "I was hoping you'd lie to me."

"I kissed you because I was jealous," he stated bluntly. "And because it's all I've been thinking about doing since I can remember." Before she could go on, which was likely going to be a scathing mouthful, he continued, trying to inject some humor to pacify her. "We've got bigger problems than you overly enjoying my kiss, though."

"Cocky, much?" she muttered, yet they both knew he was right, and her lips did curl up a wee bit though she tried to hide it. She slanted a look at him, still noticeably flustered. "What's going on?"

"My magic isnae working," he began but stopped short when a light rap came at the door.

"Adlin," she whispered, shocking him that she instinctively knew such. But there was something to that wasn't there? In fact, when she opened the door to his father, he realized he was in her mind even more than before, catching far more thoughts. In turn, he suspected she was catching his too hence knowing it was da.

"Adlin!" She smiled and embraced his father. "So glad you're here!"

There was no missing the concern in her eyes because she was with Tiernan when it should have been someone else. He embraced his father next and started to explain himself, but da cut him off.

"Och, nay, 'tis not to worry about right now, Son." His eyes flickered from the sword to Tiernan. While he knew his father tried to speak telepathically, nothing came through. "'Tis lucky for ye I saw the sword's light and found my way here because ye vanished from my mind." He shook his head. "'Twas a bloody unsettling feeling and has your ma in an uproar."

No doubt it did.

"What do you mean, vanished?" He frowned then finally took in his father's attire. "And what are you wearing?"

"The robes of my calling," da revealed. "Something I havenae had the opportunity to wear in this lifetime until now." He eyed his robe over, quite pleased. "'Tis good it found me again." He chuckled, referring to his prematurely white hair. "Everything matches just as it always did." His eyes lit up, as he snatched an ancient-looking gnarly stick out of nowhere. "I even got my cane back!"

As it happened, his father was the incarnate of the original Adlin, who first started Clan MacLomain hundreds and hundreds of years ago. He had been an immortal white wizard born from Ireland into

Scotland. Based on his attire, it seemed his former life was catching up with him.

Once upon a time, MacLomain wizards occasionally wore the robes of their calling. White wizards wore white robes and worshiped the Christian God. Black wizards wore black and worshiped the old gods. Some were Christian, others pagan. They were all good, though. Just able to access different magic.

Adlin, as he had always been, was the most powerful of them all.

"I dinnae ken." Tiernan shook his head. "Why did I vanish from your mind, Da? How did you find me?" He narrowed his eyes and spoke telepathically yet knew da didn't hear him. So he spoke aloud. "I cannae sense you anymore either. 'Tis truly unsettling."

"'Tis," da agreed, not answering Tiernan's questions. He eyed the place before narrowing in on the bed. "There's not much room for sleeping, aye?"

"That's what I said," Julie kicked in.

"I dinnae suppose that bothers my son overly much, though," da murmured. His fond eyes returned to Julie. He went on as though he hadn't just said he knew his son wanted to sleep with her. "How are you, lassie? It's been too long. At least for me."

"I'm good," she replied, then answered what she imagined would be his next question. "Everything's good in New Hampshire too. All the Brouns are there…well two are, three are on the way."

"Yet none of them are here," he remarked. His gaze went from Tiernan to the pendant he had given Julie. "'Tis a lovely bauble, lass." When he fingered it, and magic flickered briefly in his eyes, he knew his father sensed Tiernan's magic in the jewelry. "Verra special."

"It is," she agreed, glancing at Tiernan. "It was thoughtful of Tiernan to give me something when he knew my friends were getting the rings."

"Aye, 'twas," da said softly. His knowing eyes met Tiernan's. While he thought for sure his father would comment on the unique magic of the pendant, he did not. "Things have grown worse at home, lad. Your cousins' magic fluctuates more by the day." He sighed. "Not surprisingly, Cray and Marek are faring worse than the lot of them." He looked skyward. "That, naturally, has Clan MacLeod in an even worse uproar than your good ma."

"Ah, the dragon-shifter MacLomains," Julie murmured. "Their inner dragons must be going nuts."

"They arenae happy." Da's curious gaze landed on Tiernan. "But we've even more pressing matters than that, aye?"

"I couldnae leave her behind, Da," he said softly, assuming his father referred to Julie. "Surely, you knew that."

Julie's eyes widened a little. "What do you mean, he knew that?"

"I'm his da, lass," Adlin reminded. "Of course, I knew he was in love with you."

She pressed the heel of her palm to her forehead. "This is crazy."

"Aye," da confirmed. "Love can indeed be that."

Baffled, she looked at him. "Aren't you concerned that he feels this way?"

"Not really," he replied. "'Twas bound to happen between you eventually." He shrugged. "'Twas only a matter of time."

"It's not *between* us." She shook her head. "It's totally one-sided."

"Och, lass, 'tis unlike you to lie." Da chuckled and winked at her. "You love Tiernan every bit as much as he loves you."

"I held him as a baby," Julie exclaimed. "Not to mention, the mega elephant in the room that should be addressed right away." She shook her head. "I'm not a Broun!" Her eyes rounded. "I'm a...watcher-over-of-houses-for-time-travelers."

"That's a mouthful," da mentioned.

"It really is," she agreed.

"Mouthful or not, you're far more than that, lass," da said. "You always have been."

"I agree," Tiernan added.

"Well, I wouldn't go that far," she muttered. "But, thanks."

"Why wouldn't you go that far?" da asked.

"Because all I do is watch over houses," she reminded. "That's my thing."

"Lass, you've not only watched over houses but single-handedly managed a flight of ancient dragon-shifters during one of our Viking ancestors' wars," da reminded, clearly impressed. "Dragons that traveled through time forty-five thousand years and had to settle in the twenty-first century for a while." He shook his head. "No easy task, but you did it," he gave one firm nod, "and you did it well."

Tiernan hadn't even been born yet when that happened.

"I just did what I had to do," she said absently, forever humble. One of her countless attractive traits.

"Why did you do all that, though?" da said softly. "Why did you go back and forth between houses all for something you could never be part of?" He gave her a pointed look. "Not the way you truly wanted to be."

She shrugged a shoulder. "Because you and Grant asked me to."

Da pondered that, curiosity once again in his twinkling eyes. "Did we?"

"Well, yeah…" She frowned, confused. "I think."

"I dinnae recall asking you any more than Grant does, lass." Da patted her on the shoulder affectionately. "Not to say we werenae grateful."

"You must have asked me." She kept frowning. "Why else would I have been there?"

"As you now know, or should I say *remember*, because you were supposedly cousin to the first lasses who traveled back in time to ancient Scandinavia," da replied. "Though they never could recall growing up with you." He shrugged. "Then, of course, you helped Sean O'Conner along in finding his true love."

"Right," she murmured, confusion on her face as she tried to get to the root of things.

"Whilst you might have been subjected to a wee bit o' Scottish wizardly magic," da went on, "'twas only ever supposed to bring you into the fold whilst Viking Kol found his love." He shook his head. "But ye just kept returning all on your own, and fell into the role of protector of time-travelers." He grinned. "'Tis a more snappy title, aye?" He thought about that. "Or mayhap simply time-traveler protector."

Julie went to reply but snapped her mouth shut.

Her thoughts floated through Tiernan's mind.

Adlin's got to be joking. How could I just show up out of nowhere? I had a life…didn't I? Hell, what was my life? I hung with Viv for a time, but what else? Where did I come from? Why can't I remember?

Sensing she was close to panicking, Tiernan urged her to sit and thanked his father when he handed over a skin of whisky.

"'Twill be all right, lass." Tiernan crouched in front of her and urged her to drink. "We'll figure this out."

"Aye, there is truly a bit to figure out too," da commented, peering out the crack in the door. "Best to do so elsewhere for now, though."

Surprised, he glanced at his father. "You want us to leave young David?"

"Grant's spirit is around," he assured. "He will let me know if we need to return. Besides, we willnae be gone for long."

"Grant's here?" Julie exclaimed. "Where?"

"Flittin' about David for lack of a better word," da replied. "He's the only one who can be around the wee king all the time without being seen."

"Right," Julie murmured, her troubled expression unchanged. "Adlin, I need to know what's going on because I'm getting all sorts of signals." Her eyes met his. "Why aren't you more upset that I'm here? It makes no sense." She shook her head. "None of this does."

"Nay," he concurred. His kind eyes stayed with hers. He joined them and rested his hand on her shoulder. "I agree, a lot of this doesnae make sense, but one thing does." His gaze flickered between her and Tiernan. "You being here with my son, and I will tell you why."

He said more, but Tiernan couldn't hear him. The Viking sword suddenly crackled with lightning, flashed white, and thunder crashed.

What happened after that revealed how truly strange things had become.

Chapter Seven

ONE SECOND SHE was standing in front of a regal-looking chair, the next, white light flashed, and she was surrounded by tall standing stones. Seconds later, the light faded, and Tiernan pulled her close, evidently of the mind to protect her.

"What's going on?" she whispered. They were outside now. Sweeping green hills lay on the horizon, and glittering blue water was off to their left. "Where are we...where were we in between?"

"We *were* at Westminster Abby," Adlin murmured from nearby, having traveled with them. His troubled gaze narrowed on what looked to be a small, chambered tomb at the center of the standing stones. "We are *now* on the Isle of Lewis in the Hebrides. More specifically, at the *Fir bhrèige*, or the Calanais Standing Stones."

"How," Tiernan began but seemed to realize as he eyed the sword sheathed at his side. One that hadn't been there before but leaning against the wall in the cottage. "The blade brought us then?" He frowned at his father, putting the pieces together. "So from the Monastery of Scone where the *Stane o Scuin* used to be to Westminster Abby where it reportedly was when David was crowned." He looked around warily and didn't release her. "To here."

"What is the *Stane o Scuin?*" she asked. "And why did I see a chair along the way?"

"The *Stane o Scuin* is the Stone of Scone," he revealed. "Or Stone of Destiny."

"Or as the Sassenach call it, The Coronation Stone," Adlin muttered, still eyeing the tomb. "There is an odd feeling here that I

43

dinnae recall from the past." His gaze went from the sword to the stones. "'Twas almost as if our ancestors' magic latched on to something and whisked us this way…mayhap."

"What sort of something?" She pulled free of Tiernan because he was clearly content having her right where she was. "What does Viking, or should I say dragon magic, have to do with a coronation stone and standing stones?" She eyed the Stonehenge, curious. "And why was the Stone of Destiny moved?" She frowned, mulling everything over. "And again, what was with the regal chair?"

"The stone was moved because it was stolen," Adlin said.

When Julie looked at Adlin in confusion, Tiernan explained.

"In our Lord's year, twelve hundred and ninety-six, the Stone of Destiny was taken by Edward I as spoils of war. He brought it to Westminster Abbey, where it was fitted into the chair you just saw." He frowned, clearly not impressed. "'Tis now known as King Edward's Chair on which English sovereigns are crowned." His expression soured even more. "'Twas essentially Edward's way of claiming his status as "Lord Paramount" of Scotland, with the right to oversee its king."

"I had always hoped the rumors of monks hiding the real stone in River Tay were true," Adlin remarked. "Hence, tricking the Sassenach into taking a substitute." He shook his head. "But I sensed the stone in that chair." His eyes narrowed as if he were trying to understand something just out of reach. "Or at least I think I did."

"Is the stone still there in the twenty-first century?" She might be concerned that she was here on someone else's adventure, but that didn't mean she wasn't still curious. She really did enjoy history.

"Actually, 'tis quite the story behind the stone." Tiernan grinned. "On Christmas Day nineteen fifty, four Scottish students removed it from Westminster Abbey. Regrettably, during the process, it broke into two pieces. So after burying the greater part of the Stone in a field, they camped out for a few days until everything calmed down then eventually made it to Scotland."

"With a new accomplice named John Josselyn," Adlin added. "Ye cannae forget him."

"Nay," Tiernan agreed. "According to an American diplomat posted in Edinburgh at the time, the stone was hidden for a short time in a trunk in the basement of the Consulate's Public Affairs Officer, unknown to him, before it was removed."

"Aye, 'twas cleverness at work," Adlin went on. "Though English, Josselyn, who was then a student at the University of Glasgow, was a Scottish Nationalist. In fact, ironically enough, Edward I was Josselyn's twenty-first great-grandfather. Anyway, the smaller piece was similarly brought north at a later time. The entire stone was then passed to a senior Glasgow politician, who arranged for it to be professionally repaired."

"So essentially," Julie said, "Edward's own descendant helped return what his ancestor had stolen?"

"Precisely," Tiernan confirmed. "A search for the stone was ordered by the British government but proved unsuccessful. In nineteen fifty-one, the custodians of the stone left it on the altar of Arbroath Abbey, in the safekeeping of the Church of Scotland."

"Unfortunately," Adlin continued, "once the London police were informed of its whereabouts, the stone was returned to Westminster."

"Well, that's crappy," she exclaimed. "It was Scotland's to begin with!"

"Aye," Tiernan agreed. His eyes twinkled like his father's. "All was not lost, though, because it *was* eventually returned. Yet rumors still circulate that a copy had been made of the stone and that the Sassenach didnae get back the original...which means it might still be out there somewhere."

"So the stone," she said, "or *a* stone, whether it's the real deal or not, is back in Scotland in the twenty-first century."

"Aye, due to a growing dissatisfaction amongst the Scots, 'twas finally returned in nineteen ninety-six," Adlin confirmed. "'Twas transported to Edinburgh Castle, where a handover ceremony occurred. Prince Andrew, Duke of York, representing Queen Elizabeth II, formally handed over the Royal Warrant transferring the stone into the safekeeping of the Commissioners for the Regalia. It currently remains alongside the crown jewels of Scotland, the Honours of Scotland, in the Crown Room."

"That's assuming," she said, "the real stone was returned in the first place by the Scots."

"Aye," Adlin murmured, a twinkle in his eyes. "That's assuming."

"If the real one is still out there somewhere in Scotland," she cocked her head, perplexed, "why not return it now?"

"There could be many reasons," Adlin replied. "It might be held by an avid black-market collector or someone that doesnae trust it in the hands of officials or," a strange light entered his eyes, "it could be held by Scots of my ilk. Wizards determined to keep it out of the wrong hands."

"Because it possesses magic," she surmised.

"Aye," Adlin said reverently. "A great deal, I'm told."

She gazed around. "How does the Stone of Destiny tie in with this place, though?" She gestured at Tiernan's blade. "And the Viking sword."

"I dinnae quite know yet," Adlin said softly. He crossed his arms over his chest and kept eyeing the tomb though he spoke to Tiernan. "What do you make of this, Son? What do you feel here?"

"I dinnae know how dependable anything I feel is right now."

For a split second, her foolish heart sank before Tiernan continued.

"Except for the way I feel about Julie."

She seriously needed to stick to her guns, but it got harder by the moment. Especially seeing him here in his element, surrounded by rolling fields and a stunning landscape. Nevertheless, eye on the ball. She needed to return to the future. So she hung back and gave him space. Or should she say gave herself space, because the more she was near him, the more difficult it became to remember she wasn't allowed to be with him.

And that kiss hadn't helped any.

That amazingly unbelievable, entirely too perfect kiss.

She should have pulled away, stepped back, turned her head, but no, she just went with it. More like, totally lost herself in it. Every fiber of her being had been wrapped up in the way he'd made her feel. She hadn't stayed strong and broke it off. She hadn't held her ground in the least.

No, she simply surrendered the moment she had the chance.

"'Tis a verra unusual feeling around the stone, Da," Tiernan agreed, standing beside his father, clearly relieved that his magic was sensing something at all. "A mix of energies, aye?"

"Aye," Adlin replied. "Whilst there's good, there's also bad." He frowned. "Something took place here recently."

"Something ceremonial by the feel of it," Tiernan murmured. "Something interconnected…"

When he trailed off, the oddest sensation rolled over her. She swore she saw a spark of bluish-green light come from her pendant before Tiernan's sword began to glow.

"Um…guys?" she whispered, almost afraid to move because she didn't want to be thrust through time without being a whole lot closer to Tiernan first. "Are you seeing what I'm seeing?"

"'Tis your sword again, Son," Adlin said softly. "'Tis aglow but softer this time."

Thankfully, Tiernan was by her side in an instant, in case they were shifted again. Yet nothing happened.

Until it did.

"Oh my God," she whispered when transparent streams of soft light became obvious. One went from her to Tiernan's sword to each and every stone before it shot up into the sky then branched out in several directions, vanishing on every horizon.

She gazed up at the sky. "What am I looking at?"

Tiernan and Adlin looked at the sky as well, perplexed.

"What *are* you looking at, lass?" Adlin asked. "Because I dinnae see anything."

"Nor I," Tiernan concurred. His gaze dropped to her pendant. "Except for that."

"What?" First, a chill swept over her, then it almost felt like static electricity. She followed his line of sight only to realize the light from Tiernan's sword wasn't directed at her but her pendant. "It's glowing!" She shook her head, baffled. "But that's not what I'm talking about." She gestured at the line between them then swept her arm around, encompassing the sky. "I'm talking about the cobweb of lines over us. Surely you see them."

"Och," Adlin exclaimed. He closed the distance and fingered her pendant. "It cannae be."

"What cannae be?" Concern for her darkened Tiernan's eyes. "Tell me what's going on, Da. Is Julie in danger?"

"Nay," Adlin whispered, awed. "She is part of what protects us from danger."

No sooner did he say it than a boom resounded and pure hell unleashed.

-A Scot's Pledge-

Chapter Eight

HE TOOK UP arms in front of Julie when what looked to be three well-armed monks appeared beside the tomb. Though he and da threw magic at them, they somehow deflected it. Not an easy task against two arch-wizards. But then their magic wasn't at its best.

"Stay back, Jules," he roared, attacking the monk warriors alongside da with weapons instead.

Unfortunately, the monks were as talented at fighting as they were with magic.

He fought one, da the other while both battled the third on the side, crossing blades with absolute precision. Yet he knew right away he had the advantage with the Viking blade. Something they seemed to know too because all three focused their magic on it. A darkness similar to what he had felt near the tomb.

After slashing one man's arm, Tiernan swung and nicked another's thigh before he leapt forward and kicked the side of the third man's knee. The monk roared in pain, unable to dodge Adlin's sword thrust through his neck.

"Watch out," Julie cried.

Tiernan spun and ducked beneath a blade, then went to block another sword coming at him only for it to hit an unseen wall inches from his neck.

He blinked, trying to make sense of what was happening. A soft bluish-green haze had formed around him connected by a transparent line to Julie's pendent. He frowned, confused. He had cast a spell on it to protect her, not him. So why was it doing the opposite?

His father chuckled with delight muttering something about a protector indeed before he drove his sword through the baffled monk trying to attack Tiernan. The other warrior scrambled back, vanishing where he had first appeared.

"Bloody hell, I didnae want him to escape," da grumbled. "But, he was quick." He eyed the sky. "And had the advantage."

"And why is that precisely?" Tiernan said. The light around him retracted back to Julie's pendant before it snapped away altogether.

"I'll explain once we get back to the castle," da replied. "We must let the others know what's going on."

Tiernan and Julie glanced at each other curiously then frowned at da when he simply stood there and looked between them rather than chanting them home. So Tiernan started to chant only for his father to put up a hand and shake his head.

"I want to see something, Son." He looked at Julie, quite sure of himself. "What were you thinking about before we were whisked here by the blade? Back in the cottage at the Monastery?"

"You know what I was thinking about." She frowned. "The same thing I'm still worried about now. Me being here when it's supposed to be one of my friends."

"So, at root, Tiernan's safety?"

"Well, Scotland's too," she replied. "Everyone's for that matter if Tiernan doesn't hook up with his Broun."

"But it all breaks down to my son's safety, does it not?" Da considered her. "More than it has anyone else that you've helped over the years." Kindness meant to put her at ease, lit his eyes. "'Tis all right to say, lass. 'Tis okay to put one above all others."

"Because he's your son," she said softly, clearly not sure if she should put it so bluntly.

"Because he's the man you love," da corrected. "You can only ever put him first...right from the verra beginning."

Rather than comment on that, she deflected. "Why do I get the feeling you're getting at something specific?"

"Because I am and 'tis well past time I share it."

When Tiernan looked at his father in question, da revealed far more than he anticipated.

"'Tis a little known fact about arch MacLomain wizards that from the moment their eyes connect with their parents out of the womb, their magic flares for the first time," he informed. "Though it exists within the womb, it typically lies dormant. 'Tis a bit of a failsafe to hide them from those who might mean them harm."

"Interesting," Julie murmured. "Dragon magic is obvious right from the point of conception."

"Dragons are a different breed altogether," da reminded. "Anyway, as it so happened, Tiernan was not like other arch-wizard infants. For his eyes never glowed when they met ours, nor did his magic flare. In fact," his voice dropped an octave as though he were telling a great secret, "Milly and I were fairly certain he wasnae a wizard." He shook his head. "We didnae think he possessed any magic at all."

"Really?" Julie's eyes widened a little. "That must have been shocking...and disappointing."

"Nay, we wouldnae have been disappointed," da chastised. "He was our lad, and that's all that mattered." He shook his head again. "He didnae need to possess magic to be a good man. To do good things in life."

Though warmed by his father's words, he was more than baffled.

"How do I possess magic now, then?" Such as it was in its fluctuating state. "I dinnae ken."

"As it turned out, you were a late bloomer," da informed. There was a curious, fond look on his face when he gazed at Julie. "More than that, 'twas not our eyes that first sparked your magic but another's."

"You've got to be shitting me," Julie whispered. Her thoughts swirled with his. How adorable she had thought Tiernan was when she held him for the first time swaddled in his MacLomain plaid. How charmed she'd been by the way his little eyes flared with blue magic when they first met hers. "It was...with me?"

"'Twas," his father said softly, looking between them. "I knew then that though you werenae a Broun 'twas important that I took Tiernan to visit you over the years." Da seemed quite convinced. "You shared a connection that I felt should be nourished." He winked at Tiernan. "With yer good ma's full support, of course."

"To what end, though?" Julie looked from Tiernan to da, unmistakable pain in her eyes. "Why would you promote this when you knew it was impossible...because you *were* promoting it weren't you? Not just a friendship but something more?"

Da eyed her for a moment before he relented on a sigh. "Aye, I was." He looked from Julie to Tiernan. "'Twas…and still could be," he admitted, "a verra heartbreaking decision for all parties involved, but I didnae want to see love lost to obligation and honor. All the things that can stand in the way of two people being happy."

"'Twas because of ma," Tiernan murmured, suddenly understanding. "Because of what happened betwixt you in your previous life. Because of your obligations to Scotland and destiny, you lost nearly a whole lifetime with her before you could spend those last few years together."

"Aye," his father whispered, his eyes pained. "I knew from the moment your magic flared in Julie's arms, something great existed betwixt you, and I didnae want you to suffer the same pain I did." He looked from Julie to him again. "You loved her from the verra beginning, Son. It just took on several forms until it became what it was supposed to be."

"What about me?" Julie said, at last, blissfully blunt. "Did you ever think about *my* heart in all this? That in all essence, I'm you in this story, Adlin? That destiny says Tiernan has to turn from me." Fresh pain saturated her eyes. "That I have to watch him love another like I know you did Mildred in your last life?"

"I *did* think of you, lass." Guilt flared in da's eyes. "And whilst, aye, you're right, you are me to a degree, our circumstances were much different." He shook his head. "Either way, I prayed God would bring you together. That He would find a way." He glanced from Tiernan to her. "And I believe God has." He shrugged a reluctant shoulder. "Well, in truth, both He and the old gods." His steady gaze settled on them both. "'Tis no small thing for a mere mortal to spark an arch-wizard's power, and now I'm beginning to suspect why."

"Why?" they said at the same time.

"Because she is your sworn protector, Son." Adlin looked between the two, seemingly over his guilt and quite pleased with the situation. "Julie was, in a way, born of both the new God and the old gods."

Chapter Nine

Argyll, Scotland
1346

JULIE HAD NO chance to respond about her potential godliness before the sword, and her pendant wrapped them in bluish-green, white light. Everything vanished only for something she had long dreamed of to appear.

"Now *that*," Adlin declared, grinning, "had nothing to do with protecting you, Tiernan, and *everything* to do with Julie starting to accept that she might belong here after all."

"Oh, *wow*," she whispered, staring at the sprawling castle surrounded on three sides by sparkling blue water. Teary, she took in the various turrets, wall-walks, double moats, and portcullises. "That's it, isn't it?" She glanced from Tiernan to the castle. "That's your home…MacLomain Castle."

"Aye, lass." Tiernan squeezed her hand. "Welcome home…at last."

"I'm speechless," she whispered, pointing out the falsity of her statement. "Well, you know what I mean." She smiled at him for a moment forgetting everything else going on. She never thought she would live this moment. That she would stand here with him and finally see the castle he spoke about so fondly. "Thank you."

His eyes softened. "For what?"

"For…I dunno…this." Her gaze drifted back to the castle. "For pushing me to come long enough that I at least have this moment…I'll always have it."

"'Twas you who brought us here," Adlin said softly. "'Twas your magic that made sure you had this moment, lass."

"There you are," came a woman's exclamation. "I knew I sensed you!"

"Milly!" Julie smiled and embraced Tiernan's mom when she appeared out of the woodland. "It's so good to see you again!"

"I couldn't agree more." Milly held Julie at arm's length and looked her over with approval. "Look at you. More beautiful than ever." She winked. "And looking fabulous in a medieval dress, by the way."

"I don't know about that." She chuckled. "Alas, I had no choice thanks to being whisked through time."

Which brought her mind back to precisely where she was.

More so, what Adlin had said before they ended up here.

"Oh, dear, I know that look," Milly murmured, clearly seeing the weight settling on Julie's rhetorical shoulders. "We best get her back to the castle, Adlin, so you can explain whatever it is you just told her."

Milly blew her son and husband a kiss, took Julie's hand and pulled her along past a gorgeous towering Oak tree in front of the castle.

"I don't belong here," she began only for Milly, who had obviously been filled in telepathically, interrupted her.

"You definitely belong here, sweetheart." She squeezed her hand. "I think you belonged here long before now."

"You do?" Both his parents were so confident? "Aren't you worried that I'm not a Broun?"

"I think 'tis best we bring her to my chambers," Tiernan said. "Before she meets everyone."

Well that just got kinky.

"To talk," Tiernan said into her mind, amused. *"For now, anyway."*

When she glanced over her shoulder at him, he winked.

"After all," he reminded, *"there's a cot at the monastery waiting for us to spoon."*

Strange as it was to hear a medieval highlander say that, he made her smile.

Adlin appeared to be ready to do as Tiernan suggested and magically whisk them inside, but she stopped him.

"Though I'm super eager to understand what you meant back there, Adlin," she said, sure his magic was out of whack too, and that he must be wrong, "I'd really like the experience of entering the castle like everyone else." She shook her head. "No magic."

"Then you will have your experience," Tiernan assured before his father could answer. He took his mother's place and held her hand. "But you will walk in with me."

"As friends," she warned.

He grinned. "Friends who hold hands."

While she could argue it out with him, she'd really rather not. If she were only ever going to do this once, then she would damn well do it the way she'd dreamt it. With him, holding hands if that's what he wanted. Probably for the best actually out of all the possible scenarios. Because the way she'd always pictured it was silly. Something out of a romance novel.

The moment she thought it, she cursed because seconds later, she was swept up in his arms.

"Put me down, Tiernan," she exclaimed. "This is ridiculous."

His grin blossomed into a smile. "Why?"

"Because I'm not some damsel in distress," she muttered. She gestured at the drawbridge he carried her over even as she admired it. "Nor do I need to be carried over the threshold, so to speak."

"You werenae the only one who wanted it to be like this the first time," he informed. "Now, we're both getting what we wanted." He winked again. "And despite your protests 'tis clear enough you verra much like it."

Damn her traitorous thoughts.

"This is silly." Yet she settled in to enjoy the ride and admire the scenery rather than bicker with him.

Until he dropped his next bombshell.

"'Twill be a fitting story to tell our wee bairns someday," he said. "'Twould not have been right for me to merely walk you along."

"Children?" she hissed quietly. She peeked around his shoulder to see if Adlin and Milly had heard him. They might be looking elsewhere, but they obviously had based on their smirks. "Damn it,

Tiernan." She rounded her eyes at him. "That's it, put me down. I'm letting you get away with far too much!"

"Soon, lass," he assured, strolling casually beneath the second portcullis when he should be striding. Naturally, they were earning plenty of interested stares from people passing. No wonder. Their laird was carrying a strange woman over the bridge.

"Besides," he went on. "'Tis only right, I carry my sworn protector into my castle for her first visit."

"Oh, no." She shook her head and wiggled for him to put her down, but he was far too strong. "You are *so* not carrying me all the way into the castle."

"Well, you *did* say threshold," he reminded, his smile firmly in place. "The end of a drawbridge is not a threshold."

"Technically, I said a 'threshold, so to speak," she grumbled. "Which means not quite a threshold."

"'Tis not one at all." He chuckled. "I will put you down once you're over the threshold." He shook his head. "So you might as well enjoy being carried as much as I'm enjoying carrying you."

"M'Laird," a tall, smokin' hot Scotsman said. He fell in step alongside them as they entered the courtyard. With chiseled, swarthy good looks, he could only be Graham and Christina's son. "You're back sooner than expected, Cousin." He grinned at her, a hard-to-read look in his light green eyes along with recognition if she didn't know better. "And you're not alone."

"This is my cousin, Ethyn. Acting laird in my absence." Tiernan did not put her down for proper introductions. "Ethyn, this is Julie."

"'Tis good to finally meet you, lass." Ethyn's grin only grew. "I cannae say I'm surprised that you're here instead of a Broun."

Though tempted to sigh and scowl at Tiernan, she didn't want his family to think she was a bitch. So she smiled warmly at Ethyn and made sure he understood she wasn't allowed to walk on her own two feet. "I'd shake your hand, but Tiernan's being stubborn and won't put me down."

Ethyn's brows swept up. "Is that right?"

"Aye," Tiernan confirmed, giving it right back to her. "As soon as I see through what she envisioned for her first visit and secretly longed for so she could be close to me, then I will set her down."

Ethyn's smile grew wider still. "Secretly longed for, aye?"

"Aye." Tiernan winked at him. "'Tis one of her more mild longings so 'tis no hardship."

His cousin chuckled. "Nor would her less mild longings be either, aye?"

"Hell," she muttered, figuring these two out quick. Better watch what she said around them because joking seemed to be their preferred language.

"You just missed Rona and Colmac," Ethyn informed Tiernan. "Rona sends her regards."

"Who are Rona and Colmac?" she asked, taking in the courtyard and everything Tiernan had talked about over the years. The stables, armory, warrior's quarters as well as numerous cottages. MacLomain Castle had expanded its wall years ago to encompass more villagers. The times were growing especially turbulent, and the more clansfolk inside the wall, the better. Now with their magic fluctuating, she could only imagine.

"Rona is a second cousin," Tiernan replied. They started up the stairs to the castle. "She recently married Colmac MacLauchlin, who's in charge of MacLauchlin Castle until Laird Keenan returns from war."

"Which, rumor has it, will be soon," Ethyn enlightened.

"Aye, good," Tiernan replied. "Colmac has done verra well seeing to his clan since the illness but 'twill be good to have Keenan and his brothers about to help bring things back to what they once were."

"Aye," Ethyn agreed.

"'Twas around the time of Rona's return that our magic started fluctuating," Tiernan revealed to Julie. "She, like any without magic, no longer remembers that magic exists. That her own clan possesses witches and wizards. That we always have."

"Oh my God," she whispered. "I knew it was bad, but not that bad." She looked at Tiernan and frowned. "Why didn't you tell me sooner? This just proves how much you need a Broun hook-up!"

"Aye, it seems we all do," Ethyn concurred, opening the castle door for them. "And, as requested, we're all here to discuss it."

All? Seriously? Sure as heck, when they entered the great hall she had long imagined being carried into, three men standing in front of the fire turned their way. Though she wanted to admire the massive nautical tapestries, especially the Viking tapestry, as well as the monstrous mantle with its numerous faces, all she could focus on were them.

Stranger yet, she almost *felt* them for lack of a better description.

All were damn handsome, and all were tall, broad-shouldered, and perfectly muscled. One had short dark brown hair, startling light turquoise eyes, and wore the Hamilton plaid. That could only be Aidan, Grant's great-grandson. The other two were undoubtedly MacLeod dragons.

While she had dealt with Sigdir dragons before, what she felt when these dragons' eyes locked on her was entirely different. Alarming. Seconds later, a low growl rumbled in both men's chests.

Tiernan tensed and held onto her tighter.

Bright blue light flared in his eyes, signifying his magic had ignited.

If all that wasn't enough, the blonde strode right up to them, his fiery dragon eyes flaring with possessiveness, his words ground out. "She belongs with a dragon, Tiernan."

More alarming still, her bubble of bluish-green magic didn't wrap around just Tiernan now, but encompassed them all.

Chapter Ten

"STEP ANY CLOSER, Cray," he warned, never more serious, "and ye will find out precisely what an arch-wizard can do to a mere dragon wizard."

His magic might be fluctuating, but he'd find a bloody way to keep Julie safe from his cousin. Even if he had to lay down his life to do it. He knew Cray was unstable because of what was going on with their magic, but that mattered little right now. All he cared about was keeping her out of harm's way. He conveniently set aside that her magic seemed determined to keep Cray safe in turn. He also set aside that he himself was off-kilter and responding with anger rather than reason, which was out-of-character.

"*Mere?*" Cray's dragon eyes flared with rage. "Ye bloody—"

"Enough, Brother," Marek bit out, clenching his fists, clearly trying to keep his distance. "*Now.*"

"Aye." Tiernan narrowed his eyes at Cray, moments away from setting Julie aside and attacking. Again, jealousy ruled his emotions, but he couldn't stop himself. "Ye best listen to yer laird, Cray, and ye best do so straight away."

Meanwhile, Julie's blasted light that he thought was only for him pulsed around him *and* his cousins. Interestingly enough, his parents had entered but were observing rather than interfering.

"Back off." Julie frowned at Cray, not intimidated by him in the least. But then she'd had plenty of practice dealing with dragons. "I'm not a Broun, so I won't end up with any of you." She went on, making Tiernan happy indeed. "And just to be clear, if I were meant for anyone, you can bet your ass it would be Tiernan." She narrowed her eyes at his cousin. "So should we start over, Cray MacLeod? My name's Julie, nice to finally meet you."

His typical scowl firmly in place, Cray narrowed his eyes right back. "Ye're bold."

"When it comes to dragons, yes," she replied. "Especially dragons like you."

"Dragons like me?" His brows flew together. "What is that supposed to mean, lass?"

"It means, as I'm sure you already know because you're not typically this much of a dick," she replied, earning a chuckle from the others, "that I've dealt with enough Sigdir and Ancient dragons to have come across a few like you."

"And what am I like?" he growled.

"Angry initially," Julie informed. "But probably the most fiercely protective of those you love once you simmer down." She shrugged. "Which says something because dragons are instinctually protective creatures."

Cray crossed his arms over his chest and considered her for a moment before he came to a decision as quickly as he could take to anger. "You are respected by the dragons you have dealt with, aye?"

Interestingly, as his anger simmered down, Julie's protective barrier faded.

"I *am* respected, actually," she confirmed. "But then, I respect them in turn." She winked. "Dragons tend to like that."

"Aye, she's got you figured out, lad." Aidan chuckled then introduced himself, kissing the back of her hand despite her still being in Tiernan's arms. He gave her his name, which she seemed to have figured out anyway. How could she not with this particular cousin?

"'Tis nice to finally meet you, lass," Aidan said. "I have heard a great deal about you."

Tiernan had always been closest to Aidan. He sensed it was due to their connection to Adlin and Grant, who were equally close, having apprenticed together in one lifetime or another.

"I've heard a lot about you too, Laird Hamilton." Julie smiled. "It's nice to finally meet you." Her gaze swept over the others. "All of you, for that matter." Before they could respond, she went on. "Just so you all know up front, and hopefully understood when I was dealing with the younger dragon, I'm not here to try to steal a Broun's place. I'd never do that, and Tiernan knows it."

Stating Cray was the younger of the two dragons earned her another chuckle from all but Cray. It had been a fine way of pointing out that his youth was to blame for his actions because his brother had behaved much better.

"Tiernan brought me back in time without asking," she continued, assuring them this was temporary. "And I'm working on getting back."

"Wishing you the best of luck with that," Aidan said, amused, taking in her current position in Tiernan's arms, his double meaning clear. "I dinnae think Laird MacLomain intends to let you go now that he has you."

"As astute as ever, my lad," da said, finally joining the conversation. "Nor, do I suspect, he's meant to."

It hadn't gone over his head that the great hall had cleared out because his father had subconsciously nudged everyone along. Had Tiernan been thinking clearly, he would have done the same, but he'd been too focused on protecting Julie from Cray.

"Please, everyone sit," da went on. "There is much to discuss."

"Telling news, I hope," Marek grunted. "My dragon grows tired of being repressed." He gestured at his brother. "'Tis putting us all in a verra foul mood."

"Repressed?" Julie said, surprised. "So, you can't shift?"

Marek shook his head. "Nay, not since whatever this is began."

"I'm sorry to hear that." She gave Tiernan a pointed look, reminding him that he had accomplished his goal. "I think it's safe to say I'm officially over the threshold."

Not of my chambers, he nearly said but knew they needed to focus on the matter at hand. So he reluctantly set her down, keeping her close and away from the dragons when everyone sat at the head trestle table.

"Now that I've caught everyone up telepathically about what happened at the stones," da announced, clearly glad his magic had allowed him to do such, "I think the first thing we should discuss is Julie herself." Tankards of whisky were set down for everyone. "More specifically, what I discovered about her at the *Fir bhrèige*." He sat across from Tiernan and Julie. "Something confirmed not only when Julie's magic brought us here to this castle, but when it protected all of you just now."

"I don't have magic," she muttered, yet she was as curious as everyone else to hear what da had to say.

"You *do* have magic, Julie," da corrected. "You have a great deal of it." His kind eyes remained steady on her. "And whilst it could be said you're a late-bloomer like Tiernan, it wasnae quite like that."

Da gestured at Tiernan, but his gaze never left Julie. "Where my son's magic was sparked by true love, yours was, as I suspected, triggered by the need to protect him." He put up a finger to stop the others from interrupting. "Dinnae mistake my words for saying you dinnae feel precisely the same love for him, Julie. 'Tis true indeed. Otherwise, this would be impossible." He shrugged. "You simply did not need magic sooner."

Da appeared to consider his own revelation then spoke before anyone could get a word in edgewise. "I *am* inclined, however, to say your dormant magic most certainly helped you oversee things in the future over the years, Julie."

"Da," Tiernan kicked in before his father's thoughts led him down various paths as they could often do. "Mayhap 'tis best to stay on track for now?"

Da frowned. "I am staying on track."

"Somewhat, dear." Ma patted da on the shoulder and sat beside him. "Perhaps you're thinking out loud some?"

"Was I then?" He shrugged and grinned at his wife. "I tend to do that more with the years, aye?"

"Certainly more as you come into who you were always meant to be," she conceded, offering da the smile that made his eyes light up more than usual. "Luckily, I loved the man you were in our last life as much as I do this one." She tilted her head in Julie's direction. "Now stop making the poor girl wait. Tell her what's going on."

"Aye, then." Da grinned at Julie. "Simply put, lass, you're a Guardian Witch."

She chuckled, obviously thinking he joked. "A guardian *what*?"

"Witch," Tiernan provided.

"Yeah, got that," she said slowly. "Just...not really sure..." Her brows pinched together. "What's a Guardian Witch?"

"A witch," Ethyn reminded, grinning.

"Oh, stop you two," ma chastised. She shot Tiernan a look that told him they better stop joking around or else.

"Sorry, lass," he said into Julie's mind. *"We're just trying to keep things somewhat light for you."*

"I know." Her eyes flickered to his. *"But I'm with your mom on this."*

"People usually are," his father mused, hearing their telepathic conversation just fine now it seemed.

"To put it more simply," his father said aloud, continuing his explanation. "A Guardian Witch is the only living creature born with the blessing of the old gods and the one true God." He eyed Julie, impressed. "You're essentially harnessing a very old and rare power born of a time when gods set aside their strife and wanted all their people watched over." He sighed. "For as it stands, many religions do not protect those who dinnae believe in them."

Julie went to speak but instead took a swig of whisky. Then another and another.

Meanwhile, his father continued.

"Honestly, I thought Guardian Witches no longer existed." He rounded his eyes at ma. "They werenae even around way back when I created my Defiance." His eyes widened further. "Even when the Celtic gods delivered me to Scotland."

He noticed his father had been mentioning his Highland Defiance more often of late. It had been a magical building he'd created in his last life. A place to bring pagans and people of the Christian faith together in unity. Unfortunately, it hadn't gone as he had hoped, so he began the MacLomain clan instead, encouraging his kinsmen to believe in whatever deity they wished whilst living in peace.

"Yet it seems Guardian Witches do still exist," his mother replied to da, her eyes kind as they went to Julie, who had now downed half her mug. "It will be okay, sweetheart. You're not going through this alone." She gestured at everyone, then Tiernan. "My son, above all, will be by your side every step of the way. He, like all of us, has been through the awkwardness of navigating our magic for the first time."

"Aye, and he, above all, will most certainly see to you, and you will see to him," da said. "After all, once a Guardian Witch connects with he she is sworn to protect, the bond is unbreakable and eternal."

-A Scot's Pledge-

Chapter Eleven

THOUGH WELL AWARE she was catching a buzz, it didn't stop her from taking another swig of whisky. Adlin had to be wrong. He just *had* to be.

"So you're saying I'm some sort of a…guardian angel…" she managed, "yet technically a witch?"

"That is *precisely* what I'm saying." Adlin nodded, pleased. "You are the culmination of divinity and paganism."

"Uh, huh," she murmured. To hell with girly swigs, she downed the rest of the mug in one long swallow. "And I'm bound to Tiernan for life?"

Oh, but if that were only true. Then it occurred to her she might be bound to watch over him while he loved another woman. That would just flat-out suck.

"Aye, you're bound to him for life." Adlin smiled. "'Tis every bit as much a bond as the MacLomain-Broun connection." He turned his grin on Milly. "See, I told you I was right about them being meant for each other."

Meant for each other. Not her watching him love another. If only.

"And I told you I agreed they were meant for one another," Milly reminded Adlin, once again gesturing at Julie. "Now, don't get distracted. Tell the girl all of it."

"Right, aye, then." Adlin focused on Julie again. "Mind you, I only know so much about your sort of magic." He shook his head. "Which means I cannae tell you everything because it wasnae

65

something that existed in my time. Nor were rumors about it overly informative."

"Of course not," she muttered, stealing Tiernan's mug. "Just lay what you know about me on the line, then I guess I'll go from there."

Because Adlin was definitely serious despite his lighthearted nature.

Which meant if he said she possessed magic, then she did.

"Or..." She narrowed her eyes, not sure she should get her hopes up, however scary possessing magic might be. If it meant being with Tiernan, she'd deal. "What if what you think I am is all part of your magic fluctuating, and isn't true?"

"You saw ley-lines, did you not?" Adlin asked. "Then, you saw how your magic protected Tiernan in battle?"

"You mean the pendant *he* gave *me*," she reminded. "Which I'll bet he put a protection spell on." She was about to say more when it occurred to her what he'd led with. "Did you say *ley-lines*?"

"Aye," Adlin confirmed. "You know what they are then?"

"Yeah," she replied, going with one of her many theories. "Hypothetical lines stretching from Stonehenge to Stonehenge across the world." She snorted. "But those are just made up."

When Adlin perked a brow at her and shook his head, she sighed and said, "So not made up?"

"Nay, lass," he said. "Our magic tells us they exist, but to the best of my knowledge, they have never actually been seen by anyone." He gave her a telling look. "The confirmation that ley-lines are actually visible was once handed down from Guardian Witch to Guardian Witch. Eventually, the witches were no more, but the knowledge lived on."

Adlin looked at her with admiration. "As far as I know, Guardian Witches, *you*, are the only ones who have ever seen them." He cocked his head in consideration. "'Tis also said ley-lines dinnae just connect Stonehenges but holy places too. 'Tis a combination of the old gods and new." He gestured at the MacLeods. "That is why you could manage dragons so well in the twenty-first century, then just now attract them as you did."

She narrowed her eyes slightly at Cray, with his tattooed blonde chiseled good looks, warning him not to start again then peered at Marek curiously. With black hair, and a scar on his temple that only added to his fierce handsomeness, it made sense he was the chieftain of his clan. Though all the turbulent emotions common to a dragon shifter simmered beneath the surface, he had learned to manage his exceptionally well.

"Why is that?" she asked Adlin, focusing on Tiernan's dad again, not quite getting it. "What's my connection to dragons?"

"Their ancestral gods," he replied. "Whilst most MacLomain's have Norse ancestry, dragons such as Marek and Cray have closer ties to our Viking ancestors due to their inner beast. Which means closer ties despite who they might worship now, to the Norse gods our ancestors worshipped." He gestured at the non-dragon wizards. "Then, of course, some worship the Celtic gods."

"And of course the one God," she murmured, knowing full well which deity Tiernan paid homage to.

"Aye," Adlin confirmed. "Interestingly, from what I witnessed at the Stonehenge, it seems the Viking magic in the sword is also interconnected. To what end, I havenae figured out, though 'tis safe to say 'tis working in our favor."

"What about Tiernan's cousins?" She frowned. "Why did my magic, which might I remind you came from the pendant Tiernan gave me, protect them?"

"From what I've heard," Adlin replied, "your power will protect any who would die for he you are sworn to protect," he rolled his eyes at Cray, "despite their behavior."

"Why didn't it protect you at the Stonehenge then, Adlin?" she asked. "Because you'd definitely die for Tiernan."

"Mayhap because it had just ignited and was still adjusting," Adlin theorized. "Or because whoever those monks were affected it somehow."

"So should I assume that for whatever reason, the source of my magic comes from this pendant?" She fingered it and sipped more whisky. "Because beyond some weird sensations here and there, the obvious stuff comes from this."

"I think that and whatever is going on in Scotland helped spark your magic," Adlin replied. "Yet, I suspect the strange sensations you're having are more directly connected to what exists within you."

"So, how am I supposed to use it?" She frowned. "Control it?"

"As time goes on, 'twill become clearer, lass," he promised. "Though haphazard at times, magic tends to work itself out. 'Twill show you the way." He gestured at everyone. "Plus, as Milly said, you have all of us to help you the best we can." Then he looked at Tiernan. "Most especially, my son."

"Right," she murmured, her head swimming a little from the whisky. "Who I should stay with through this, I take it? Or should I go home and let my friends know what's going on?"

"Unfortunately, outside of your new magic," Tiernan said, "we still dinnae know what's going on."

"We are, however, one step closer," she said softly, sure of it though she had no idea why. "We know those monk warriors initially did something at the Calanais Stonehenge that left dark magic behind, likely somewhere around the tomb." She met Tiernan's eyes. "And we suspect they're manipulating the magic of the ley-lines to travel around Scotland."

Pride lit Adlin's face. "Aye, you're catching on fast, lass."

"Aye," Tiernan agreed, just as impressed. "Your magic will guide you more and more."

He put his hand over hers, in comfort, and she was grateful. Sure, it was a little cool simply *knowing* things out of the blue, but it was also jarring and discomforting.

"Julie, you said back in New Hampshire you felt Balliol's disinherited nobles were at the root of this," Tiernan continued. "Do you still feel that way?"

"Absolutely." She'd never been surer. "I don't know if they're the same men or working alongside them, but those warrior monks are definitely tied in with the nobles."

Adlin nodded. "Then we have a sense of direction." He looked at the others. "We also have the daunting ongoing issue of our fluctuating magic." He shook his head. "That I couldnae even connect with my son was beyond troubling."

"Aye," Marek agreed. "The same sort of thing is happening with us dragons."

"Which must tie in with not being able to embrace our inner beasts," Cray added.

"Oh, you did okay with that," Julie teased, well aware the liquor was at work.

Cray, in turn, didn't quite smile at her, but he didn't scowl either. She'd call that progress.

As to be expected of dragon males, especially ones who descended from the MacLomain's Sigdir line, he and his brother were clearly a force to be reckoned with. It would be interesting to see which of her friends were meant for them because from what she'd seen over the years, being with a dragon was a unique experience.

Her eyes slid to Tiernan. Yet here she was possibly meant for an arch-wizard. An experience she suspected would far outdo unique.

"So, Grant is watching over David whilst you are here?" Aidan said, interrupting her thoughts.

Now there was a lady killer with his enchanting eyes and sexy dimples. Where Ethyn seemed quickest to humor she suspected under his contemplative, steadfast nature, Aidan was fairly lighthearted too. But then he'd have to be to get along so well with Tiernan.

"Aye, Grant watches over wee King David," Adlin confirmed. "Though 'tis best, Tiernan and Julie return soon."

"Mayhap I should join them," Aidan offered. "'Twould do my heart good to see great-granda again, such as he is."

"What of your clan?" Milly asked. It was clear she liked the idea of him going along. "Will they fare well without you?"

"Aye," Aidan assured. "Da's seeing to them just fine."

She had heard good things about his father Conall and his mother, Lindsay, a former Hollywood actress. Hopefully, she'd meet them before this was all over. She'd also love to meet Marek and Cray's parents, Bryce and Jessie, but time would tell. Best that she didn't get too far ahead of herself and assume she might be able to stay. That she might be able to be part of all this. To finally settle down somewhere and call it home.

"Might it not be prudent for all of us cousins to go along with Tiernan and Julie?" Ethyn proposed. "Or mayhap some of us should go to the future to find our Brouns before 'tis too late, and we might not be able to time travel?"

"I think it's already too late," Julie whispered, trying to pinpoint the odd sensation washing over her. "Something about those stones…"

"Och," Adlin murmured. His eyes flared with magic when they connected with hers. "Whatever they're doing to those stones is the same thing that's affecting our magic…" His brows flew up in surprise. "Yet, it makes yours stronger by the moment."

"Because I can still travel," she whispered, sensing the ley-lines, seeing them as though she still stood in the circle of stones. "I can travel along them, can't I?"

"Aye," Tiernan murmured, sounding certain.

But then he was in her mind.

She glanced at him, jolted by the sudden sensation she had.

"You're...in me somehow..." she said. "In a different way than just hearing my thoughts and telepathic words." She took another sip, never taking her eyes from his. "What *is* this feeling?"

Adlin cocked his head, considering them, more so Tiernan. "What does it feel like, son?"

"Like...love," he whispered, clearly trying to narrow it down more. He shook his head. "But stronger if possible..."

"It sounds an awful lot like what Brouns and MacLomains feel when the magic of the Claddagh ring ignites," Milly mentioned.

"Aye," Adlin agreed.

"It also sounds like mating," Cray muttered, his anger back, his pale brown almost golden eyes turbulent.

That's when she felt it. Cray's recent loss from the illness that swept through Scotland. Not just his but Aidan's too. A woman. She had been their best friend. Both fell for her. Aidan was somewhat coping, but Cray wasn't doing well at all.

"Oh hell," she whispered, looking at him, sucked into a tunnel of certain knowledge. "You need your dragon back more than most, or you're never gonna make it, Cray."

Then she felt more and looked at Aidan. "And while you might be coping and doing what's expected of you, holding onto the devotion you felt to her will only destroy any future love before it has a chance to begin." She shook her head. "And you can't just *pretend* to love your Broun as you intend to do...or *can* you...is that possible?" She scowled. "It better not be because that would be so unfair to whichever one of my friends you're meant for."

Just like that, she whipped out of the tunnel vision she'd been in. The sensation was so jolting she would have fallen over backward if Tiernan hadn't put an arm around her shoulders and caught her.

"Aye," Adlin said, awed, understanding even more. "A Guardian Witch indeed, watching over not just he who she is sworn to protect but those who stand by him."

"This is just pure crazy," she managed, taking a few hearty swigs of Tiernan's whisky. What the hell was going on? Sure, she'd always wanted to be part of all the time travel and love, but she wasn't so sure about the magical angle. Not anymore.

Cray went to say something, his expression sourer than ever now, but Adlin stopped him with a sharp shake of his head. "We must give her time to adjust." His eyes shot to the other men. "Until such time, you will accept what she says graciously. Do ye ken?"

"Aye," they replied, some with more assurance than others.

"We should tell Julie and Tiernan the last bit, Adlin." Milly sighed. "No, actually, just I should."

Oh, shit, there was *more*?

Milly looked at the others. "If you'll excuse us?"

Whatever it was required everyone to *leave*? This couldn't be good.

When Adlin looked at Milly in question, she nodded firmly. "God, yes, husband, you need to leave too. The poor girl doesn't need Tiernan's father here for this part."

"Sonofabitch," Julie muttered, then flinched, definitely tipsy. She gave Milly an apologetic look. "Sorry...you're not a bitch...and I wasn't talking about Tiernan."

Milly chuckled and waved it away. "You're allowed to curse your heart out right now, dear. This is a lot." A grim expression settled on her face once everyone was gone. "And I fear it's going to get a bit worse...or should I say more confusing."

Julie and Tiernan glanced at each other in concern.

"What is it, Ma?" Tiernan asked, his arm still around Julie.

"Well, it's a bit awkward, but someone should inform you two of one other thing about Guardian Witches." She looked between them before her gaze focused on Julie. "More so, their virtue...or, to be specific, purity."

"Purity?" Julie mouthed. "Tell me you're not talking about what I think you are."

"I am," Milly confirmed. "It's said that Guardian Witches were only ever virgins. Worse yet, that they could never lay with he who they protected." Sadness settled on her face. "For if they did, their magic would be no more and the man more vulnerable to harm than ever before."

71

-A Scot's Pledge-

Chapter Twelve

"BLOODY HELL," HE cursed and frowned at his mother, his brogue thickening with his distress. "Surely, ye jest."

"I wish I did," she replied softly, just as upset as they were because she knew how much he loved Julie. Not to mention, she wanted grandchildren. "But that's what they say. You're not supposed to sleep with your protector."

"Slow your roll," Julie said, slurring slightly. She was in her cups, and he didn't blame her. "For starters, as you well know, Tiernan, I'm *not* a virgin." She hiccupped. "So that settles that end of things."

"I bloody well know ye're not a virgin," he muttered, keeping her steady lest she teeter back again. He focused on his mother. "She makes a good point, though. If she's not a virgin, then the rules have already changed."

"They have," his mother agreed, quick to optimism. "Your father and I just wanted you to have all your facts upfront."

"Meaning you don't think it's such a good idea that we sleep together," Julie said bluntly. She didn't need to be in her cups to say precisely what was on her mind.

Which turned out to be more than he expected.

"So essentially," Julie went on, "our coming together, if that's what you want to call it, works the opposite of everybody else." She scowled. "If that is, we go off the premise that any of this even applies to us."

Ma's brows perked in a mixture of amusement and concern as she figured out Julie's vague words quicker than him. "You could only be referring to MacLomains and Brouns growing more powerful once they lay together."

"Actually, I was thinking about dragon mates, but yeah, sure, that." Julie sighed and took another swig before her eyes met his. "Just when I thought there might be hope for us, we've got the red light again."

He was just glad to hear there had been a green light to begin with.

"To hell with that." He downed her whisky, which was really his, and said exactly how he felt while at the same time trying to lighten her mood. "Besides, there isnae electricity in medieval Scotland."

"So, no red light." The corner of her lip curled up. "Very funny."

"True, though." He shook his head, refusing to allow her to get too down or worse yet, to entertain the idea that this might be true. That they couldn't lie together if she meant to protect him. He looked at his mother again. "Julie is no longer pure, yet her magic still protects me. So things are verra much different." He tilted his head in question. "Might it be possible that our magic is combining? That lying with me would make her stronger like it would have had she been a Broun?"

"I would say your magic will let you know and 'tis not something to fret over at the moment," his father said, returning right on time. His gaze flickered over Julie, taking in her quickly deteriorating state before his eyes met Tiernan's. "Meanwhile, 'tis best, you and Julie get back to wee David."

"Have you heard from Grant then?"

"All is well." Adlin gave Tiernan a pointed look. "'Tis just time to get a good night's rest, then think things over on the morn, aye?"

"Aye, Da." He prayed his magic worked enough to get them back because Julie's magic would undoubtedly be askew right now. He embraced his parents. "We will see you soon. Hopefully, with more news."

"All three of you," Adlin replied moments before Aidan returned. "'Tis best you take your cousin along. When your magic works, it tends to complement each other's as mine and Grant's once did."

"Aye," Tiernan agreed, happy to have Aidan along. "Mayhap 'twill increase our odds of getting where we need to go too."

Julie said nothing to that, but then her eyes were already half-mast.

"It's going to be okay, Julie," his mother said as she and Adlin embraced her. "I don't doubt it for a second." Ma looked between Tiernan and Julie. "Not when it comes to you two." She offered a warm smile. "And mothers tend to know these things."

Julie didn't offer a response, but her state was indeed worsening by the moment. Not only was she not used to whisky, but he suspected her igniting magic had amplified its effects. She needed to lie down. So whether she liked it or not, he scooped her up again and off they went. Regrettably, as they soon discovered, things were most certainly growing dire. It took not just Tiernan and Aidan's magic but a nudge from his parents as well to return to King David in thirteen thirty-one.

"Bloody hell, I dinnae like the feel of this," Aidan muttered, lighting a fire on the hearth by hand rather than with magic. "I feel emptier by the day."

"Aye," Tiernan agreed, glad to see Julie had already passed out.

He laid her on the bed, covered her, then simply watched her for a lingering moment. His heart ached for her struggles. For all that had been thrown at her today. He even acknowledged his part in it. How he hadn't given her a choice. At the time, it had felt so right and still did, but that didn't make it any easier for her.

"I might not be connecting with you too well telepathically," Aidan said, "but I know that look on yer face." He urged Tiernan to sit in front of the fire with him and handed him a skin of whisky. "Ye feel like ye've contributed to all she's been through here." The corner of his mouth shot up. "And ye have, Cousin." He grasped Tiernan's shoulder and shook his head. "But 'twas the only way it could have gone. Ye had to follow yer heart at long last."

He appreciated the support, needing it more than he realized.

"She's right, though," he said softly. "'Twas poor of me to put what I wanted before kin and country. To think only of my desires and not how it might affect her."

"Ye *were* thinking about how it would affect her," Aidan replied. "Because ye know she deserves the kind of love ye feel for her. She deserves more than the lonely life she was living." He shrugged. "As to kin and country, it seems we need her more than anyone right now, so bringing her back in time was downright heroic."

"'Twas selfish and ye know it."

Aidan grinned. "That too." He shook his head. "Ye know full well 'tis a rare day things dinnae happen as they're supposed to for those of us with MacLomain blood."

"No truer words were uttered," came a disembodied voice before a welcome presence appeared.

"Great-Granda," Aidan exclaimed, smiling warmly. "'Tis always a welcome thing to see ye but frustrating not to be able to embrace ye hello."

"Aye," Grant agreed.

Having manifested beside the fire, he smiled warmly at them both. While transparent, his visage was easy enough to see. He had appeared as a young man with his Hamilton plaid wrapped proudly, making the striking family resemblance between him and Aidan obvious.

"All is well with wee David," Grant assured. "He sleeps soundly."

"'Tis good, Uncle." Tiernan nodded hello. "'Tis also bloody good to see ye."

Grant nodded in agreement before sharing that he'd been to see Adlin, and he was all caught up. Then he shared some interesting, albeit alarming news of his own.

"Unbeknownst to them, I have visited Balliol and his nobles," Grant divulged. "They talk about war and rightful lands but little else of consequence." He shook his head. "As far as I can tell, they arenae connected with the warrior monks. Not to say that's cut in stone. They still might be in a way I've yet to ken. For I discovered unusual things along the way that leave me with more questions than answers."

Tiernan perked a brow. "Along the way where?"

"From Stonehenge to Stonehenge, starting at the one you visited earlier."

"And?" Aidan prompted when Grant momentarily ceased speaking. His ghostly body drifted as though caught in a draft coming off the fire before he manifested again.

"I've never seen ye do that before." His cousin frowned. "Is everything all right?"

"Aye," Grant muttered. "'Tis just the affect all of this is having on my ethereal form. It requires more energy than usual to remain this way." He shook his head. "The elements dinnae always help either."

"Och, so whatever's affecting our magic is affecting the afterlife too?"

"A wee bit here and there but 'tis not to worry about at the moment." Grant eyed the men. "The bigger issue is what I discovered on my travels. I was able to track the same dark energy ye sensed at the tomb to five other locations."

"Which ones?" Tiernan asked.

"The Ring of Brodgar in the Orkneys," Grant began. "The Stones of Machrie Moor, The Kilmartin Glen stones, and the stones at Clava Cairns."

"That's only four," Tiernan murmured, sensing he wasn't going to like the next Stonehenge in the least.

"Salem," Julie suddenly gasped. She bolted up from a sound sleep. Her eyes shot to Grant. "The darkness is at the Salem Stonehenge too. It's at Mystery Hill in the twenty-first century."

-A Scot's Pledge-

Chapter Thirteen

"SALEM," SHE MURMURED on a yawn. She rolled over, cuddled against warmth, and inhaled the scent of spicy perfection, whispering, "Tiernan," because it reminded her of him.

"Aye, lass," he rumbled.

Her eyes flew open before she shut them to blinding light. What the heck? She wasn't in the twenty-first century but…where the hell was she?

"Are we traveling through time again?" she rasped, parched. Her tongue felt like sandpaper. "So blasted bright."

"Nay, we're not traveling through time." He chuckled. "'Tis raining out and verra dim."

"Really?" She cracked open an eye, only to realize she was snuggled up against him. That's when it all came rushing back. Guardian Witches, evil monk warriors, and oh yeah, no sex allowed for the virgin she wasn't.

Even worse? It all boiled down to one hell of a hangover.

"Fuck," she whispered and pressed the heel of her palm to her forehead. "What the *hell* was I drinking?"

"Good Scottish whisky." His eyes were a bit too merry for her taste when they met hers. "And a fair bit o' it at that."

"Oh, man," she groaned. "I don't drink like that. *Ever.*"

Well, mostly ever.

Her stomach flipped, and nausea swelled.

"Oh, crap." She stumbled from the bed, mortified but also a little thankful when Aidan opened the door for her and recommended she go around back.

So she did, just in the nick of time too. While she wasn't crazy about puking around Aidan, it wasn't the first time she had around Tiernan. He had popped into the future once when she had the flu. Suffice it to say he'd helped her through quite a bit that weekend, holding her hair back when she was sick and feeding her homemade soup.

Once she had spent herself, she plunked down against the side of the cottage, be damned the wet ground. She wasn't surprised to find Tiernan standing there, holding a blanket over her head so she wouldn't get too wet. He handed a skin out to her and urged her to drink. "As you twenty-first century Americans say, a hair of the dog that bit you, aye?"

"Good God no," she groaned, covering her nose against the foul-smelling whisky that had tasted pretty damn good yesterday. She gestured at the other skin he held. "What's in that?"

"Water." He handed it to her. "Though the other would help you find your feet again."

"Good thing I'm fine right here on my ass then." She downed half of the refreshing water in two long gulps, then rested her head back against the building and closed her eyes. "I'm gonna have to find another way to de-stress because this seriously blows."

"I can think of a few ways." He grinned and winked. "Ways that will feel much better than the effects of whisky both the night before and the next morn."

"Lord, how can you even think about sex right now?" She held her forehead, thinking about sex just fine actually. In fact, thinking about that helped her not think about her pounding head.

That is until she remembered they weren't allowed to be intimate.

"That is not precisely what ma said," he murmured, clearly catching her thoughts. "Nor is it something I intend to listen to."

"You will if I do," she said softly, mainly because it hurt to talk too loudly. "I can't think about this right now, Tiernan."

Because it would break her heart.

"I got some bannock for you, lass," Aidan said, peeking around the corner. "'Twill help settle your stomach."

"Somehow, I doubt that," she replied but allowed Tiernan to help her up.

Inside she found bread, soup, and more water waiting for her on a small table. She sat when Aidan graciously pulled out a chair for her.

"Thank you," she murmured, embarrassed that she was in this condition in front of Tiernan's cousin. Especially considering how close they were. Aidan was like a brother to him. She supposed, though, the time to have worried about appearances or a good first impression would have been before she got drunk yesterday. So it was what it was at this point.

"My pleasure, lass," Aidan said in response to her thanks.

"That's not good," she commented, watching Tiernan stoke the fire rather than flick his wrist like usual. "Is your magic on complete sabbatical then?"

"It comes and goes." He sat across from her. "Dinnae worry about that right now." He gestured at the bannock and soup. "Just try to get some food in your stomach. You havenae eaten since this all began."

He was right. She hadn't. So she did her best to get a few nibbles down, which, thankfully, did make her stomach feel a bit better. Once he saw she was somewhat on the mend, Tiernan caught her up on everything she'd missed while passed out.

Specifically, Grant and his latest news.

"I sat up and said Salem?" She frowned, recalling that she'd murmured the same thing when she awoke. "I don't remember doing that last night."

Way to black out. How much whisky had she drunk? One swig too many obviously.

"'Twas verra brief," Aidan provided. "Then, you promptly laid down and went back to sleep."

She could tell by the small grin hovering on Aidan's face, that he was just being nice. It hadn't gone that smoothly, and she suspected she knew why. She flinched at Tiernan. "Tell me I didn't snore."

She rarely tied one on, but if she did, she snored horribly. Like a foghorn, according to Tiernan. He would know too because he'd celebrated her last birthday with her, during which she over imbibed. Not just because he'd made the occasion so much fun but because she couldn't tell him how she really felt about him. In retrospect, drinking—truth serum that it could be—probably wasn't the best idea, but luckily, she never revealed the truth. She did, however, introduce him to her obnoxious passed out snore.

Now, it seemed, Aidan and Grant had the misfortune of hearing it as well

"You didn't snore," Tiernan said dutifully, biting back a grin.

She narrowed her eyes, smirking because she couldn't help it. "Liar."

"In truth, 'twas a series of hiccups," he conceded. "Followed by snoring." He finally gave in to a grin. "'Twas quite charming in its own way."

She outright laughed at that, knowing full well there was nothing charming about her snoring. Thankfully, the guys laughed as well, not put off in the least.

"I need to go back to New Hampshire then," she exclaimed, at last focusing on the matter at hand. More so, that her magic had evidently sensed trouble at the Salem Stonehenge. "We all do to protect my friends."

It didn't matter that she'd sensed yesterday that they couldn't. They should still try.

"Actually, we need to keep an eye on wee David," Tiernan replied. "Grant will watch over your friends and let us know if we're needed. Keep in mind as well, 'tis best to assume the monks can track us via the Salem Stonehenge."

"Which means they might know who's coming and going," she said. "Then, where we go from there."

"That's right," Aidan said. "So, the less they know, the better until we've figured out more."

He was about to continue when pounding came at the door.

As it turned out, it was time to leave.

"Thomas provided us horses," Aidan informed after stepping outside and speaking with the man who had knocked at the door. "I'll go see that they've been made ready for travel."

"I have a few changes of clothes for you, lass." Tiernan put a satchel on the bed after Aidan left. "In here."

"So no magically whisking me into a dress anymore either, eh?"

"I'm afraid not." He offered her a wry grin. "I could try, but I dinnae trust my magic to clothe you appropriately."

She chuckled. "And how do you think it would dress me?"

"'Tis hard to know." His lustful gaze swept over her, and his grin remained in place. "Mayhap in nothing at all."

Heat flared under her skin that had nothing to do with being hungover. The way he looked at her made it clear she was going to have a fight on her hands if she bought into the virgin protector thing. What was she supposed to make of that news anyway? Would magic tell her what she could and couldn't do with him? What was allowed?

Either way, she knew one thing for certain. "Nothing's happening between us until I know for sure it won't affect your safety, Tiernan." She gestured that he turn around while she changed. "You must know that."

"We'll see."

She heard the frustration in his voice and understood it. Hell, she felt the same way.

"We won't *see*," she replied firmly, pulling off her dress. "What's the big deal anyway? We've waited this long. What's a little while longer?"

Yet she knew as well as he did that a little while would feel like a lifetime.

"It could be far longer than a while," he grunted, his brogue thickening with emotion, his patience as tested as hers. "I dinnae want to wait on the whims of magic and rings anymore. I want to love ye as ye should be loved. Make ye mine in every sense of the word."

Aroused despite herself, she shook her head and stepped into a new dress. "Not at the cost of your life. It's just not worth it."

"'Twould verra much be worth it if even just once," Tiernan said softly. He was so close behind her, she yelped in surprise and nearly fell over, but he caught her.

"Tiernan," she managed, overly aware of being against him in her half undressed state. "Way to sneak up on a girl." She narrowed her eyes at him over her shoulder. "You're supposed to be turned around."

"I was." He didn't let go but trailed a finger along her jaw, his gaze lingering on her lips as though he wanted to taste them again. "But I felt what you said needed to be addressed."

"And that couldn't be done with your back turned?" *Step away, Julie. Get out of his arms.*

But she didn't budge an inch.

His eyes met hers. "I wanted to look at you when I told you how serious I was about not letting what we learned affect what transpires betwixt us." He cupped her cheek. "I refuse to let anything otherworldly dictate how we feel about each other, Julie." He shook his head. "Not anymore."

"I get where you're coming from," she said softly, under his spell despite her best intentions. "But unfortunately, the matter's out of your hands because you're definitely not the sort who would do anything without my permission."

"Except, kiss you," he murmured and leaned in to kiss her.

This time, however, she turned her lips away, firmly focused on what might happen to him if she gave in.

"Bloody hell," he growled. "Dinnae do this, lass." He shook his head. "Dinnae turn from what we share because of speculation and folklore."

"I'm not turning from it," she grumbled, pulling free from his arms. "I'm just not risking your damn life. Not gonna happen." She sighed, determined to stick to her guns no matter how hard it was. "Your parents said my magic would help me along, and I've got to trust that."

She met his eyes and spoke from the heart. "Your life's worth way more than my wants, Tiernan. I'd never forgive myself if we had sex, and I couldn't protect you anymore." She shook her head and blurted it all out. "Nothing's worth that." She searched his eyes, pleading with him. "Surely, you understand how I feel if you feel the same way." She arched a brow in question. "Would you sleep with me if our roles were reversed?"

When he scowled and sighed, she knew she had him.

"So there you go," she said softly and finished dressing.

"A kiss isnae lying with you," he grumbled, packing up the satchel.

"Yeah, right." She rolled her eyes. "I think we both know we wouldn't be able to stop at a kiss."

Amusement returned to his eyes, no doubt for her benefit. "'Tis worth a shot."

Yet she wouldn't, and he knew it.

When they departed a short while later, they were sharing a horse. That meant, as she soon learned, that he would have plenty of time to work his wiles on her. Which, naturally, he was very good at. Then again, he didn't have to try all that hard with her cozied against him.

Thankfully, the rain had stopped, but it was chilly, so he wrapped a second fur around them both, cocooning her against him.

Wickedly aroused but at the same time exhausted, she must have dozed off and dreamt because something shifted and changed. Suddenly, they were no longer riding through heavy woodland but back at the Stonehenge they had been at yesterday.

This time, however, it looked notably different.

-A Scot's Pledge-

Chapter Fourteen

"WHAT DID YOU do, lass?" he said into Julie's mind. *"I didnae feel your magic ignite."*

"I don't know," she replied. *"Pretty sure I'm dreaming, though."*

"You are," he said aloud, awed. "You are still asleep in front of me on the horse yet have somehow pulled me along. We stand at the Stonehenge together...such as we are."

"Are you asleep then?"

"Nay," he said. "'Tis bloody odd. I'm awake on the horse as we travel with wee King David yet with you at the same time. Almost as if my spirit is divided."

"Because you go where I go." She sounded certain. "I keep you with me to protect you."

"Aye." He kept her close though technically they weren't here in physical form. Or so they surmised. "It seems we've traveled back much further in time than before."

"Definitely." The stones weren't aged and weathered but freshly quarried by the looks of them. "How old is this Stonehenge anyway?"

"'Tis uncertain," he replied. "Though some speculate it was erected sometime betwixt twenty-nine hundred and twenty-six hundred BC." He glanced at her. "Verra old."

"Ya think?" Incredulous, she looked from the stones to him. "Why do you suppose we're here?"

"My guess is your magic wants to show you something." He eyed her pendant when it began glowing softly. "Something is happening."

Moments later, a line of robed women trailed out of the woodland. None looked their way, so he assumed they couldn't see them.

"Who are they?" Julie whispered.

"I dinnae know." Yet he was starting to suspect.

The women entered the circle and stopped, one in front of each stone.

"They're here to bid farewell to the sun," Julie said softly, her eyes not quite right as she watched them. As she clearly remembered. "They do this every solstice. They bid farewell to the sun then harness the special light it creates at sunset." Her eyes rose as the sun sank. "The ley-lines are appearing."

The women lowered their hoods, looked up as well, and began chanting.

"They're Guardian Witches," he said softly, certain of it.

Julie responded, but he couldn't understand whatever language she spoke. Ancient Celt if he were to guess. The sun sank lower still. Something began to happen. Change.

Suddenly, he saw what Julie saw.

Felt what she felt.

Understood what she said.

"It's coming," she murmured aloud. "Something is coming..."

As she said it, the sun hit the stones just right, and every ley-line lit up, even the one connected to her pendant. The witches slowly looked Julie's way, chanting all the while.

Though he nearly withdrew his sword, he held back. They meant her no harm. Rather, they meant to give her something. A token from the gods. He narrowed his eyes at the familiar essence engulfing him.

Magic that felt kindred.

A ley-line shot down to the tomb like a lightning bolt and thunder cracked. His blade crackled as well. Seconds later, the sun dipped beneath the horizon, and everything vanished but the stones.

"Holy shit," she whispered, blinking at him, back to herself now. "Did you catch all that?"

"Aye, though I dinnae know precisely what I witnessed." He frowned in alarm when he spied what else had happened. "Your pendant's gone."

"Oh, no." Worry lit her eyes as she searched her cleavage for it. She started to lift her hair but stopped and narrowed her eyes at the tomb. "Look…smoke…" She squinted. "I think there's something on the tomb."

She started to head that way, but he stopped her. "We just witnessed great power at work, lass. Wait until the smoke clears before wandering any closer."

"But it means me no harm," she murmured. "Somehow, I know that for certain." Her eyes met his. "I need to go get it, Tiernan. Please."

"Go get what?"

"Whatever's waiting for me," she replied softly. "Whatever my ancestors and the gods wanted me to have."

"Your ancestors," he murmured, knowing she was right.

She had descended from one of those witches.

Tiernan was tied in with it too somehow. He knew it with absolute certainty.

"Wield your sword if you need to," she said. "But it means no harm."

"Nay," he agreed. "It doesnae."

He took her hand and headed that way. Close, closer, nearly there, yet they only saw a trail of smoke coming off the rock. If nothing else were true, it had, indeed, been struck by lightning of some sort.

"There's nothing there but chipped stone," he murmured, still seeing only smoke and bits of rock.

"No, there's more," she whispered, reaching out. "I just have to trust it's there…I have to trust that it's meant for me."

"It is," he confirmed, suddenly never more sure of anything. His every instinct screamed at him that she was right. That something precious awaited her. "It has always been yours."

Julie reached out even further only for everything to snap away.

She jolted awake on the horse, and everything returned to normal. They were no longer in the past but the present. Or at least where wee David was.

"Oh my God," Julie whispered.

"Bloody hell!" He grinned at what glistened on her finger, shocked yet thrilled to see it there. "'Tis a Claddagh ring!"

Not just any Claddagh ring either but a work of art.

Gleaming platinum, its sparkling stone was the same beautiful blue-green as her magical light, and its band engraved with thistle leaves.

"Made by all five," he said softly, feeling its magical essences. "Your ancestors, my ancestors, God, the Celtic gods, and the Norse gods."

"That's a heck of a line-up," she whispered in disbelief.

"Aye," he said softly. "For a remarkable lass."

"My pendant's still gone though," she said sadly, searching her cleavage once again only to hesitate, suddenly understanding something. "You were wrong...it wasn't the power of five but six." Her eyes met his over her shoulder. "Your magic helped make it too, Tiernan. The magic you used to create the pendant. Hence the thistle in the ring."

"Then 'tis a ring that will protect you well, lass," he murmured, positive of it. "And 'tis also a ring that connects you to me as readily as the other rings will their MacLomains."

Unmistakable hope lit her eyes. "How can you be so certain?"

"How can you not be?"

Still hopeful, her eyes lingered on his for another moment, her internal war obvious before resolution returned to her gaze, and she faced forward again.

"Though I wish it were otherwise, this doesn't override what your parents shared, Tiernan." She settled back against him. "It doesn't change the fact that sleeping with you might mean I can't protect you anymore."

"Nay." Yet one thing was clear. "But it does bring us one step closer together. Because the stone's color is most certainly the shade of our two eye colors combined. Which, if I were to guess, means that 'tis only a matter of time before you receive the certainty you need." He knew he had sounded impatient earlier and wanted her to know he could handle it. That he would wait no matter how long it took. "A certainty I will gladly wait for even if it takes a lifetime."

"That's an awfully long time to go without sex," she pointed out.

"But I would," he said softly, never more serious. "For you."

Though he'd lain with a few women over the years mainly because she'd done the same with men, it still felt like he was waiting. That he'd been waiting his whole bloody life. Yet he would wait the rest of it as long as he could keep her close. As long as they weren't hundreds of years apart anymore.

"What was that all about?" Aidan trotted up alongside them. "I swore I saw the sword glow."

"Aye then?" Tiernan said, not overly surprised his cousin saw such. As it were when their magic wasn't fluctuating, Aidan was nearly as powerful as him and an arch-wizard as well.

"Aye." It didn't take long for Aidan to home in on Julie's ring. He smiled. "Bloody hell, look at that! A verra welcome sight, aye, Cousin?"

"'Tis," Tiernan replied, grinning.

The band of travelers slowed then stopped. It seemed they had made it to where they would make camp for the night.

"We'll set the tents up, hunt, then join Thomas and the wee king, aye?" Aidan said. "Twill be good to enjoy some freshly roasted game."

It was too when they eventually joined Thomas and King David in the royal tent. As always, the wee king sat quietly, his gaze astute. He might not speak as a rule, but his father's intelligence was there, taking it all in. Mostly, Tiernan noted, taking in Julie. But then she had a way with the boy, often directing smiles at the lad. Ones that earned her not necessarily a smile in return but most certainly interest.

"We should arrive at the holding late tomorrow," Thomas divulged as food was served. "But I expect scouts to meet up with us sooner with the latest news on Balliol and his miscreants."

"News will be welcome," Tiernan replied, knowing full well there wasn't much of it at this juncture.

They enjoyed a pleasant meal with the regent and king, speaking mostly of what was going on in the country. The unrest and uprisings. David remained silent but always kept a keen eye on them. It was clear he liked Thomas by the respectful way he watched him. In turn, the regent liked the lad too, never speaking down to him but as though he were his equal despite his age.

Sir Thomas Randolph and King Robert the Bruce had been close, so it was no wonder he treated David well. But then he suspected Thomas would anyway. He was just that sort of man. Doing his best for his beloved country. One that had been warring most of his life.

Hopefully, the news from Thomas' scouts on the morrow would be promising. Yet as Tiernan, Julie, and Aidan learned on their walk back after dinner when they happened upon Grant, they might be hoping for too much.

Chapter Fifteen

"IT'S SO GOOD to see you, Grant," she exclaimed, only to realize men around the campfires were looking at her strangely because she seemingly talked to thin air.

"'Tis good to see you as well," Grant replied once they were away from all the others. His gaze went to her ring, and he smiled. "'Tis a fine gift from so many." He looked from Tiernan to her, pleased. "One that binds you good and true to your lad, I'd say."

"You'd *say*." She sighed. "But don't know for certain?"

"I know 'tis a ring that brings true love together," Grant replied. "I also know with Tiernan's magic tied so heavily into it that true love does indeed exist betwixt you. Otherwise, the creation of the ring using both of your magic wouldnae have been possible." He shook his head. "The Celtic gods would never have allowed it."

"You mean my ancestors' magic was used in its creation," she corrected. "Not mine."

"'Your magic is in there too, lass," he replied. "If you cannae feel that already, you soon will."

Tiernan seemed extremely pleased with everything Grant shared.

"'Tis truly a special ring, lass," Grant went on, still studying it. "There has never been one that blended both the witch's and wizard's eye colors."

"My magic was that color when it was still in the pendant, though," she said.

"Magic sparked because of your wizard and you finding your way back to each other as you should," Grant informed. "'Tis all verra unusual but telling too."

"How so?"

"It all but confirms you two are meant to be."

Tiernan's smile only widened before he appeared curious. "Typically, the stone glows the color of the wizard's eyes. 'Tis how we know the power of true love has ignited." He cocked his head. "So should I expect it to eventually turn my eye color?"

"I dinnae think so," Grant replied. "But it couldnae hurt to look for the glow." He shrugged. "Or not as you've already seen the color shine from the pendant."

"So, there's no way to know if the stone shining confirms anything." She leaned against a tree and sighed again. "That means this doesn't necessarily override the whole protector purity thing."

"I think if anything, it confirms that your situation is different than your ancestors, Julie," Grant said. "I would almost hazard to say it was a direct message from them that you should follow a mix of their ways and Tiernan's." He shook his head. "Or I dinnae think they would have taken part in its creation."

"I just wish I could be sure," she said, not willing to risk Tiernan's safety on speculation even if Grant was the one doing it.

"You will be sure when the time is right," Grant said, sounding convinced before he focused on the reason he had come. "I dinnae know why I didnae sense it before, but something of note stirs amongst Balliol's disinherited. There is unrest in one of them that wasnae there last time." His expression grew troubled. "Yet I cannae sense if magic is at the root of it or not."

"It is," she said softly, suddenly feeling a little off. "A new kind...but very, very old."

She frowned, wondering why she had said that. Yet she was right. She just knew it.

"New but old, aye?" Grant considered her. "Much like that of the Guardian Witch, some might say. Magic new to us because we thought it long-extinct but verra much old magic to be sure."

"Maybe," she murmured, wishing she could sense more. But whatever she had just felt was now out of reach, like a memory struggling to be remembered. A wave of exhaustion overcame her, and she yawned. "Sorry, but I think I need to lie down."

"It's been a long day of riding," Tiernan began then evidently sensed more. From what she could tell, her magic had flared in his mind, then simmered down.

"Using your new magic will tax you at first," he went on, sounding sure of himself. "It will take time to adjust."

"You felt it then, aye, lad?" Grant eyed him curiously. "Almost as if her magic were your own?"

"Aye," Tiernan confirmed. "I've never felt anything like it."

"Of course you havenae," Grant replied. "But I have as have many before you." Nostalgia lit his eyes as he clearly thought about his beloved Sheila. "'Tis the power of the Claddagh ring. The power of twin souls coming back together."

"So you speculate," she murmured.

"So I know," Grant stated. He bid them goodnight and puffed away but not before warning them to remain vigilant. Danger could very well find them before they found it.

"Thomas intends to leave at daybreak," Aidan said, "so I'll bid you goodnight as well."

The Hamilton laird had been relatively quiet most of the evening, but she knew he was more often than not a contemplative sort, so it was to be expected.

"From a cot to a little tent," she noted as she and Tiernan crawled into the tight quarters erected at the base of a tree. It was set up to offer them extra protection from the cool southerly wind.

"'Twill be fine, lass." Tiernan murmured a chant, clearly relieved when his magic worked. A tiny flickering light no brighter than a candle ignited above them. He grinned at her. "Besides, I believe you promised me this at one time."

"Yeah, when you were a pre-teen and wanted to camp out next to the old oak in front of the colonial." She chuckled. "You always did have a thing for that tree."

"All MacLomains do," he reminded.

"Right, because its magic is tied in with the one outside your castle," she mused. "Lots of family history."

"Aye, 'tis a good tree," he replied. "And I appreciated you promising to build a tent next to it on my next visit."

"Yet by the time you returned, you were too big," she recalled, chuckling again. "Not to mention you were starting to make doe-eyes at me." She shook her head. "If you camped out, you were on your own at that point."

"Aye." His grin blossomed into a smile. "If I recall, by the next visit, I wasnae the only one making doe-eyes."

"Maybe not," she relented, remembering all-too-well watching a boy leave and a man return. She had known he would grow up into a hottie, it was just in his DNA, but she wasn't prepared for just how attracted she'd be to him. "I don't think I'll ever forget it."

He pulled off his boots while she did the same.

"I know I willnae." His smile remained intact, his eyes merry. "You nearly fell off the rock when you saw me."

"No, I didn't."

He chuckled this time. "Aye, you did."

"I didn't expect to see you appear at the Stonehenge," she began then trailed off when another one of those weird sensations washed over her.

"What is it, Jules?" he asked, alarmed at first, but at ease when he obviously sensed it wasn't life-threatening.

"I don't know," she murmured, lying back on the plaid blanket he'd laid out. "It didn't occur to me until just now, but that feeling I had when I saw you back then...was the same as the one I felt today." She met his eyes, wondering what he made of that. "I felt it at the Stonehenge with my ancestors, Tiernan. The same exact feeling of...warmth and wonder. Attraction."

"And what do you make of that?" He gave her a pointed look. "Because it sounds like even more confirmation that we're meant to be together."

Of course, that was his takeaway, and it made sense. Not enough for her to say what she knew he wanted to hear, though.

"It probably *is* more confirmation," she said softly. "But it's not enough, and you know it."

Though she *really*, truly wished it were.

She tried not to stare when he pulled off his shirt. Way to torture a girl who was determined to be on her best behavior. She licked her lips. He looked far too good. Way too many perfectly chiseled muscles. Yet her gaze was drawn to something she was fairly certain hadn't been there the last time she saw him.

"When did you get that?" she murmured.

Inexplicably drawn, she sat up and touched the circular tattoo on his shoulder. The moment she did, heat blew over her, and four arrow-looking shapes appeared connected at the center by a circle.

His eyes flared with magic then simmered down.

He had felt it too.

"I didnae have a tattoo there before." He ran his fingers over it, frowning. "'Tis warm to the touch."

"It is," she agreed. Her ring caught her attention. "My ring's changed." Shocked, she looked from the Claddagh ring to the tattoo then back again. "The same design just appeared on the crowned heart encircling the stone."

"We should summon Grant." He glanced from her ring to his tattoo with uncertainty. "See what he makes of it."

"How about in the morning?" God, she was tired, so she lay down again. "Neither my ring or your new tat feels dangerous to me. How about you?"

"Nay, but—"

"Please, Tiernan," she murmured on a yawn. "Just lie down and hold me already."

"Hold you?" He perked a brow in surprise. "Are you sure?"

"Positive." She could barely keep her eyes open. "I'm too tired to…"

That's the last thing she remembered saying before she dreamt of circles and stones swirling around her until they stopped moving, and she stood in the center. It was the design of Tiernan's tattoo. The same one that had appeared on her ring.

Steeped in fog cut through by moonlight, the place felt mystical. Powerful somehow.

"Where are we?" she whispered, sensing Tiernan before he appeared out of the fog and joined her in the center of the stones. "Why are we here?"

"They are the stones of my Irish ancestors." He eyed their surroundings with awe. "Yet some are missing."

"Are we dreaming again then?" she whispered, taken by the sight of him, wanting him more by the moment. Drawn in a way that was as mystical and old-as-time as the stones themselves.

She knew something was off about it, but she didn't care. Couldn't. Not with him so close. So eager. With her in a way he never had been before.

"Aye, I think we are dreaming." He reeled her close and tilted her chin up, seeing the same opportunity in this that she did. "And it doesnae matter what we do in a dream, lass."

"How do you know?" Yet she really didn't care.

All she wanted was to feel his lips on hers again.

To sink into the bliss he could bring her.

Rather than answer her, he gave her what she longed for. What she craved. He kissed her, soft at first before it grew more passionate and desperate. When she groaned, out of her mind already, way beyond caring if they should or shouldn't do this, he took advantage and hoisted her up.

"Tiernan," she moaned against his lips and wrapped her legs around his waist.

She trembled with blazing need when he pressed his erection against her. When he teased without taking. It never occurred to her that he hadn't chanted away their clothes, yet they had still mysteriously disappeared. But then this was a dream, right?

And they could do anything they wanted in a dream.

"Please," she whimpered, nearly clawing at him, almost crazed. She needed him with a borderline primal vengeance. "Now."

"Aye," came a raspy voice seconds before Adlin's voice boomed all around them.

"Wake up before 'tis too late!"

Chapter Sixteen

HE JOLTED UPRIGHT when his father's cane pounded down, and da's magic pulsed around them.

"What the hell," Julie exclaimed, bolting upright as well. Her worried eyes met his. "Are you…really you?" She looked him over concerned. "Are you okay?"

"I'm fine, lass." He put his arm around her shoulders when he saw her trembling. "We both are."

"Is your dad here? I could have sworn I heard him."

"Me too." He shook his head. "But he isnae here."

"He isn't, is he?" she murmured, clearly connected to da now through Tiernan. "What just happened?" She leaned against him, subconsciously seeking comfort. "Because if that was a dream, it was a little too real for my taste." Her eyes returned to his. "Your voice…"

When she trailed off, he frowned.

"'Twas not my voice but '*twas* me up until that last moment, Jules." He shook his head. "Dinnae doubt it for a second."

He was still aching with arousal, so he had definitely been there. Yet something else had been there too at the very end.

Something had been trying to slip through.

"So were we in…Ireland?" she said softly.

"Aye," he confirmed, not sure if he wanted to tell her what else they had been doing outside of the obvious.

"Just tell me." Her gaze stayed on his eyes. "Because I certainly wasn't in my right mind…not really."

He considered how much she could handle right now but realized she would always be better off fully informed. She should understand as much as possible. It might very well save her life at some point.

"If I were to guess," he said, "we were reenacting what brought my da into existence." He tilted his head in acquiescence. "In his previous life, that is."

Her brows shot up when she realized what he referred to. "Are you talking about the Irish king and the Druidess? His parents…" she cleared her throat, clearly uncomfortable she'd been anywhere near such, "*conceiving* him?"

He nodded. "If it makes you feel any better, 'tis not the first time something like this has happened over the generations." He frowned as he thought about it. "Except this time, stones were missing." He eyed his new tattoo, not sure what to make of things. "Come to think of it, the Stonehenge matched this."

"You're right." She traced her finger along his tattoo, lingering on the circle in the center. "We were right here."

"Aye," he murmured, sensing more.

As did she, it seemed.

"And we weren't alone toward the end," Julie murmured, her eyes narrowing. "Something tried to take you over, Tiernan." She flinched then shivered. "Something dark…" Her eyes narrowed even more. "Something trying to gain access." Her gaze focused on him again. "To what, though?"

"All of us," he murmured, certain of it. He looked at the tattoo and saw it differently this time. "Through you and me, it was trying to access what protects all MacLomains."

"Because it sensed weakness in you and me," she whispered, then frowned. "I don't understand…we aren't weak…are we?"

Though tempted to say it may be because his magic was fluctuating or better yet, because they hadn't lain together yet and come in to their fullest potential power, he wouldn't pressure her. She needed to be ready. To push past her fear that she would endanger him. Naturally, she came to all the same conclusions and undoubtedly followed his thoughts.

"This sucks." She frowned at him. "So what's the right answer? Be with you to save you or get you killed?"

"Like Grant said, you'll know what to do soon enough," he assured her, taking in the pre-dawn light. He felt like he'd barely slept.

But then, how could he when he'd had her in his arms like that? Wrapped around his waist, ready to sink onto him? "We should prepare to leave."

Because if they stayed here, he'd never be able to keep his hands off of her.

"Even though I sense he's not, are you *sure* your father's not here somewhere?" she asked. "I could have sworn."

"Nay, he managed to get through somehow, but he isnae here." He looked at her with reassurance, convinced da had not only saved them but kept them on the right path from afar. "We're getting closer to our truth, Julie. I'm certain of it."

"I hope so," she murmured.

"We are." He cupped her cheek and made sure her eyes stayed with his. "You know I willnae pressure you into anything, aye? That what happened in that dream was…a bit out of my hands."

He tried not to think about just how perfect her arse had felt in said hands. Or how beautiful she had looked flushed with desire.

"I know it was out of your hands," she replied. "No worries." Before he could pull away, she put her hand over his. "Just so you know, just so it's clear, I'm rooting for us, Tiernan." Her eyes grew misty. "I really am."

"As am I, lass." Though more than tempted to kiss her, he held back. Instead, much to his surprise and pleasure, she kissed him. It wasn't long or overly passionate but heartfelt. As was the look in her eyes when they met his again. She started to speak but stopped and shook her head. Yet he knew what she had wanted to say, and it made his heart soar.

"Pretty soon, Jules," he murmured in her ear. "Until then, I love you too."

He hesitated with his lips close to hers before he pulled away and declared it was time to leave. They had another long day ahead. When they exited, Aidan was already taking his tent down, his expression particularly troubled.

"What is it, Cousin?" he asked, taking down his own tent.

"'Tis nothing," Aidan murmured, truly not himself.

"But it *is* something, isn't it?" Julie said softly. She seemed to sense something. "You dreamt as well, didn't you, Aidan?"

His cousin glanced at her with surprise. "Aye, lass." His brows pulled together, and he looked between them. "What do you know of it?"

"Not as much as we'd like." She pulled up Tiernan's sleeve until his tattoo was visible. "This look familiar?"

"Bloody hell." Aidan's gaze narrowed on it. "I was there last night." His eyes met Tiernan's before he pointed at one of the arrows or standing stones. "I was by this one, trapped by some unseen force. Maeve called to me from the fog then another lass, but I couldnae see them." A haunted expression crossed his features. "Then something came...something dark."

Maeve was the woman Aidan and Cray had loved.

"Something similar happened to us," Tiernan revealed, remaining vague. "Only we were in the center."

Julie showed Aidan the new design on her ring, as well.

"'Tis good that," his cousin murmured. "It must be."

"It is." Julie sounded certain. "It's protection of some sort...the tattoo and the ring, tied in with my magic and Tiernan's."

"Five points," Tiernan murmured, picking up on her magic, feeling his own ignite. "Five Stonehenges."

"Four in Scotland," she whispered, her eyes different again. "Those that Grant mentioned."

"What about the Salem Stonehenge?" Aidan said. "Is it protected too?"

"Maybe," she murmured. "Because of that feeling..."

His cousin frowned. "What feeling?"

"When Julie first felt something for me other than friendship," Tiernan said. "'Tis part of all this somehow. Part of our magic."

"We're going to need to get back to the Calanais Standing Stones eventually." Her eyes met Tiernan's. "It's important somehow. I think our initial dreamlike out of body experience yesterday when I obtained my ring was trying to tell us that."

He nodded in agreement. "Mayhap, we'll do so whilst traveling today."

"Right...we'll astral project." Because that was *precisely* what they had done. She shook her head. "But I have no idea how I did that...or *if* my magic even did that."

"You did...it did." He was sure of it. "Do you still see the ley-lines overhead?"

Because he could not anymore. That had evidently been a temporary privilege. A perk of witnessing such old and powerful magic.

"Actually," she squinted at the sky in surprise, "I see them, but they're a little different today."

"How so?"

"I dunno," she murmured. "Some are just…different. A bit darker if I'm not mistaken."

Aidan looked from the sky to her. "Do any connect to you and Tiernan?"

"No, not right now," she said. "But then I'm not trying to protect him."

"Well, we cannae complain about that." Aidan swung up onto his horse. "I'm going to check on wee King David. I will see you two en route."

As it happened, they didn't see his cousin again until much later in the day. When they did, he still seemed troubled, and unusually edgy.

"What is it, Aidan?" Tiernan asked. They rode alongside him. "I sense a growing unrest in you."

Which was bloody good in its own way, considering he hadn't sensed much off his fellow wizards lately.

"'Tis hard to explain," Aidan replied. "Other than to say, my dream feels like it's consuming me." A heavier frown than he already wore settled on his face. "As though Maeve and the other woman are trapped on the other side of some unseen barrier that I cannae get beyond."

"A feeling of growing helplessness, right?" Julie asked. When Aidan nodded, she went on. "I know it's hard, but you need to ignore it." Her eyes met his. "I'm not sure how I know this, but I'm fairly positive that a dark force is trying to mess with your head."

"To what end?"

"I'm not sure. All I know is that we need to try to get past it and realize it's not real…not yet." She looked at Tiernan over her shoulder. "Because I know it's been growing inside you all day too. Except yours is more jealousy than anything else, right?"

"Aye," he replied. "All I can think about is that the dark force nearly had you. A force that felt masculine." He scowled. "'Tis sometimes hard to remember that 'twas only a dream."

"And that's what it's...*they're* counting on," she said softly. "I'd put money on your other cousins having had a dream about that circle last night too. And I'll bet they all dealt with a dark force that wasn't just one but several."

"'Twould not be good for the dragons," Aidan said. "As you saw, they are struggling more than the rest of us right now."

Tiernan nodded in agreement.

"Whoever *they* are," Julie muttered, "they're coming at us from all angles, aren't they?"

"Whoever they are," he said softly, eyeing her. Why did it almost sound like she knew who they were? Something in her tone bespoke a sense of familiarity. Yet did she even realize it? "Who are they exactly, lass? Do you know?"

"The damn disinherited." She frowned. "Or nobles, warrior monks, whatever you wanna call them."

"'Tis as you said, then. They're at the root of this." He sensed something more, though. A strong sense of certainty. "They *are* the disinherited."

"They are, aren't they?" she murmured. Her eyes turned to his again. "Not just men who felt screwed out of Scottish land but something more."

"Aye," he agreed, positive they were onto something. What that was, however, remained just beyond his grasp.

"What *was* that?" Julie exclaimed.

"What?" he barely got out before she reached over his shoulder, and grabbed an arrow moments before it pierced his skull.

Their eyes met each others in alarm seconds before the forest exploded with men.

Her magic hadn't protected him like it had before with a bluish-green light.

"But it definitely warned me," she said into his mind, tossing aside the arrow. *"And gave me the speed and know-how to catch that arrow."*

"Aye," he agreed, spurring the horse.

They needed to get to wee David.

"I think from here on out we should ride closer to him," she said. "Why weren't we to begin with anyway?"

"Because Thomas was confident there were no enemies in this area," he muttered, slashing his sword across a warrior's throat as they rushed past. "*Bloody* foolish."

"Yeah, it was." She grabbed a dirk out of his satchel and whipped it at another man, hitting him square in the forehead. "My magic's definitely at work...or you just taught me well."

He had tried whenever he visited, hoping that someday she might travel back. That she would need such skills.

"There's David," she cried, pointing to their left.

The boy stood behind a wall of warriors, oddly calm, considering his circumstances.

"Let me down," she ordered, already attempting to get off the horse.

"Och, lass, nay," he roared, trying to stop her, but it was too late. Despite slowing the horse, she slid free of his grasp and hit the ground pretty hard. He leapt off, his heart in his throat, but she was already scrambling in the lad's direction.

"Bloody hell, Cousin, what's she doing?" Aidan exclaimed, off his horse as well, sword-fighting with a man as he attempted to follow.

"Julie!" Tiernan tried to race after her, but too many men were coming at him. "Stop!"

Terrified for her, he fought like a berserker, cutting down man after man, without really seeing them. All he could see was her as she dodged left, right, leapt over a dead body, and made it to wee David before he was run through with a blade.

Instead, much to Tiernan's horror, she flung the boy aside and took the blade herself.

-A Scot's Pledge-

Chapter Seventeen

"I THINK 'TIS time you learn to fight," Tiernan announced.

"I know how to fight a little bit." Julie chuckled. *"The dragons taught me some when they were here."*

"Not nearly enough, though." He stopped and looked at her, serious. *"I know they taught you to use daggers."* He unsheathed his blade. *"But what about a sword?"*

"Nope, and you know that." She looked around. *"You seriously want to do this here? Now? In the woods?"*

"Why not?" He gestured at the stones then headed in that direction, calling over his shoulder, *"The ground is flatter at the Stonehenge. We will practice there."*

"But I don't have a sword," she called after him.

He sheathed his own and manifested another more suited to her size. *"Now, you do."*

"Then I guess I'm learning to swing a sword," she muttered, following him.

The truth was, she was fine doing whatever he wanted because it meant spending more time with him. He had been visiting New Hampshire less frequently since he'd become chieftain, and it bummed her out. She missed him. More than that, she'd developed a pretty intense crush on him despite knowing nothing could come of it. Still, she loved being around him, so why not entertain the fantasy awhile longer?

"First," he said when they arrived at the Stonehenge. *"You must learn to grip and swing it properly."*

He handed her the sword then stepped behind her, wrapping his strong arms around her to show her the correct placement of her hands.

"They should be like this." He placed his warm hands over hers and murmured in her ear, "Your grip should be firm, the blade an extension of your arms."

She tried to respond but only swallowed hard at the feel of him all around her.

"You must think only of defeating your enemy," he whispered, his voice a little hoarse. "You must..."

"Must what?" she whispered, meeting his eyes over her shoulder.

Lost, gone in an instant, her eyes lingered on his.

The moment stretched.

Consumed her.

Meant everything.

That's when she realized this wasn't just a mere crush but much more. Something brand new had blossomed between them.

Something she had never felt before.

"You must protect yourself, lass," he whispered moments before light blue magic flared in his eyes.

Seconds later, searing pain ripped through her. He wasn't behind her anymore. Rather he knelt in front of her, horrified. Full of fear when he was always so courageous.

Why was he looking at her like that?

What had happened?

Suddenly, her memory of them at the Stonehenge became the harsh reality of a sword protruding from her gut.

"Tiernan," she tried to whisper but couldn't. Warm blood trickled from her mouth. The world grew darker and darker before all went black, and everything snapped away.

"Protect yourself, lass," he whispered into her mind, almost as if the man from her past spoke to her now, protecting her from far away. From another time and place. *"Protect yourself and come back to me. Stay with me."*

Terrified not of dying but leaving him, she struggled toward his voice. Toward his presence in her mind.

Where was he?

Where'd he go?

Then she felt him all around her like she had at the Stonehenge. Part of her in a way that would never vanish. Inside her in a way he never had been before. As if his magic felt the connection, his blue magic filled her vision, driving away the darkness, and she opened her eyes.

Where was she?

What was going on?

"'Tis okay, Jules," Tiernan murmured. He pressed what felt like a cool compress to her forehead, his brogue so thick with emotion she barely understood him. "Ye're all right. Ye arenae harmed, lass."

"What?" she tried to ask, but her throat was too dry. He held a cup of cold water to her lips, and she drank before trying again. "What happened?"

The moment his eyes met hers, everything came rushing back. Him kneeling in front of her, horrified. The sword in her gut. The blood. She looked down, expecting to see a bloody bandage at the very least, but instead, she appeared completely unharmed. She touched her midriff, but there was nothing there. Not even an ounce of pain.

"'Tis a bloody miracle," he said softly. Fear warred with relief in his tender gaze. "One moment ye were dying in front of me…the next, completely healed." He squeezed her hand, knowing what she would ask next. "Wee David is well. Ye protected him like the hero ye are."

From what she could tell, they were in the chambers of what appeared to be a castle or some sort of stone building.

"I just did what anyone would." She kept inspecting her stomach, trembling. "How is this possible? I felt the blade…the blood…" Her eyes rose to his. "Then, I was with you. Not where I fell but back at the Salem Stonehenge."

"A memory then?"

"Yeah." She smiled and shimmied over on the large canopied bed. "You remember the day." She patted the bed beside her, wanting him closer, wanting the peace of his arms around her again. "You taught me how to use a sword."

"I remember." Understanding what she needed, he pulled off his boots, lay down beside her, and simply held her. "'Twas a good day. You were a fast learner."

"And you were a flirt," she whispered, closing her eyes, grateful when her trembling began to subside. She inhaled his scent, taking comfort in the safety he offered. The freedom from the quickly dwindling terror of being on the brink of death. "You were telling me that I had to protect myself, then your magic ignited." She looked at him. "I don't recall it doing that back then."

"It didnae." He considered what had happened to her. "It sounds like my magic was protecting you via a memory."

"Is that even possible?"

He brushed her hair back from her forehead, his eyes still remarkably tender. "When it comes to ye, I wouldnae doubt it for a moment."

"It didn't just protect me," she said, "but healed me, Tiernan."

"Or," he countered, "it protected you before you ever actually got wounded." His brows swept up. "Mayhap, whilst we saw one thing here, in truth, the magic was one step ahead."

"Can that truly happen?"

"As I said, when it comes to you, I think my magic is capable of anything," he murmured, tracing her jaw line. "There isnae anything I would not do to save you, Julie."

"I know," she whispered. Though vaguely curious where they were, she was unable to tear her eyes away.

"We are in the king's holding," he divulged, following her thoughts. "A bath is waiting for you when you're ready." Before she could ask him about everyone else, he went on. "All is well enough. Several died, but there are many here to protect wee David." He pressed his lips together in disappointment. "Unfortunately, however, the enemy remains at large."

"None were caught, then?"

"Nay."

For a split second, she felt like she had more answers about why that might be, but the sensation fled only to be replaced with another one entirely. Genuine appreciation and naturally when it came to Tiernan, desire. So much unchecked desire that it was getting harder and harder to think straight. She knew part of it was her body's way of trying to relieve such incredible stress, but a much larger part was simply him. What he had done for her. How he made her feel.

"Thank you for saving me," she murmured. Her concern for the king's safety took a backseat to the feelings coursing through her. The love she felt for Tiernan. "Because you did...I just know it."

"No need to thank me," he said softly.

He was about to say more, but she stopped him with a kiss. Then another.

Then several more.

"Lass, if we keep this up," he said into her mind, *"'twill be hard to stop."*

"Then don't stop," she murmured against his lips.

He cupped her cheeks and met her eyes, his brogue thickening once again. "Are ye saying what I think ye're saying?" His inner struggle was painfully obvious, but he did right by her regardless. "If ye are, then ye should keep in mind ye just suffered a traumatic experience. Mayhap ye're not thinking clearly." He shook his head. "'Twould be poor of me to lay with ye right now."

"No, it wouldn't," she said softly, searching his eyes. "Grant said I would know when the time was right, and it is, Tiernan. I knew it the moment you wrapped your arms around me in that memory." She traced her finger along his strong stubbly jaw. "Whatever blossomed between us back then fueled what happened today. The connection that formed that day was forged into something even stronger. Something made of our magic and our hearts." Her throat thickened with emotion. "It's unbreakable." She tilted her head in question. "You *must* feel it?"

"Aye, I feel it, lass," he murmured. "But then I've always felt it."

"Because you possessed magic," she reminded, positive she was on the right track. "Everything inside me is telling me the time is right. That we can only ever grow closer. That intimacy would never separate our magic...would never prevent me from protecting you."

"Though I loathe mentioning it when I'd much rather be enjoying you, I wouldnae forgive myself for not reminding you of what happened." He brushed a curl away from her eye. "Your magic seemed to falter when the arrow nearly hit me. Or at the verra least, it behaved differently."

So maybe her magic was off now was his point. But it wasn't. Not at all.

"My gut tells me that happened for the very reason your magic's fluctuating." Tired of talking, she ran her hand up under his tunic, at last, touching flesh she'd wanted to feel for so long. "Whatever's going on at those stones is looking for weakness, trying to break us down." She brushed her lips across his and met his eyes, never more sure of anything. "We need to follow the path of the Claddagh ring and get our magic under control."

She could tell by the look in his eyes that he warred with how much to argue, so she took the words out of his mouth by kissing him…then straddling him. Then kissing him some more. Soon enough, he was kissing her back, and as she hoped it would, passion made stopping impossible.

She felt like she was on a rollercoaster of sensations and emotions when he flipped her beneath him and undressed her. Not quickly but not slowly either, as though he were trying to savor the moment but at the same time, impatient. His lips followed in the wake of the clothing, sampling everything from her neck to her shoulder blades to her cleavage.

She groaned with appreciation when he lowered the material down over her breasts, fondled and kissed them. When he pulled an overly sensitive nipple into his mouth, she about came off the bed it felt so good.

"Oh God," she gasped, biting her lower lip as he suckled and swirled his tongue around an engorged way too sensitive nipple.

Everything he did, touched, kissed, fondled, felt incredible. Different than any before him. Though she could say it was because they were already close, she knew it was far more. The chemistry was through the roof. Sizzling hot. Powerful. Dizzying in its intensity.

"Tiernan," she groaned when he continued down, kissing and tasting her belly, then hipbones as he removed her dress and tossed it aside.

"Come here," she managed.

She wanted him in her.

Now.

She felt a pressing urgency. Like they were running out of time.

Yet it seemed he had other plans between her thighs. And any hope of stopping him flew out the window the minute she felt what he was capable of.

"Ohhh," she exclaimed, gripping the blanket. When he manipulated her swollen, aroused flesh with his tongue and fingers, she came hard almost instantaneously. He clearly thought he was going to settle in and continue to feast, but she shook her head. "Get up here."

She wanted to feel the weight of him, finally feel his hard body against hers, feel him deep inside her... part of her.

"Och, lass, with thoughts like that, how can I refuse ye?"

She struggled for breath, adrift in her ebbing orgasm as he whipped aside his tunic and plaid, finally revealing what she'd envisioned one too many nights with her vibrator. And damn, if her fairly vivid imagination didn't do the man justice. He was head-to-toe male perfection from his broad shoulders to his cut abs to that delicious 'V' leading to the scrumptious dick between his legs. She swore, just looking at him made her climax again.

So ready for him it hurt, she pulled him down, spread her thighs, and kissed him, desperate for more. Eager to feel everything. All that he could offer.

"Are you sure?" he murmured against her lips.

"You're asking me that now?" She rubbed against him, driving him on. "Little late for that, don't ya think?"

"I could still stop," he said hoarsely.

"No, you can't," she whispered, running her legs along his, enjoying the feel of his shaft against her wet folds. "Way too late for that."

She could tell by his expression, the pure strain and arousal, that she had him. There was no turning back from this. No stopping. Seconds later, he proved her right and pressed deep, shooting her straight into pure bliss only to be shot down a second later when a loud rap came at the door.

They had been summoned by the king and were to appear straight away.

-A Scot's Pledge-

Chapter Eighteen

"BLOODY HELL," HE cursed, loathe to move unless it was to thrust deep inside her over and over until he heard her screams of pleasure. Until he released his seed. Finally being inside her felt too good. Too perfect.

"Tell me we have time," Julie said hoarsely, in the same state as him. She trembled, her body craving his with equal fervor. "Just a few minutes. Just…more…of this." Her eyes met his. "Of you."

"'Tis unwise to keep the king waiting." Just one thrust. Just to see how much more it would transform her expression. Just to feel her sweet depths stroke him. Yet he wouldn't be able to stop at one, and he knew it.

So he said he was sorry, brushed his lips across hers, and pulled away, assuring her they would return to this soon.

"'Tis likely the lad simply wishes to thank you," he grumbled, eyeing her the whole time he dressed.

She outdid his many late-night fantasies of her from her lush little breasts, small waistline, to her curvy hips. He was pleased to discover the dusting of freckles on her cheeks and arms were also on her chest and even some on her stomach. He'd already memorized the location of every one on her front and looked forward to treasure hunting on her back.

"This stinks," she muttered, dressing. "Damn timing."

"I couldnae agree more, lass." He cupped her cheek once they were ready. "'Twill be soon enough though. Later this verra night." He shook his head and ground his jaw. "Dinnae doubt it."

Though tempted to kiss her, he knew they'd end up back in bed, so he pulled her after him, and they joined Thomas and David in the great hall. As expected, the boy wanted to thank Julie in person, and it wasn't nearly as pressing as it had seemed. Nevertheless, they had been summoned so best that they came when asked.

"Thank ye for saving my life, missus," the lad said softly, clearly struggling with shyness.

"You're very welcome," Julie said warmly.

While he knew she was drawn to the child, it was far more obvious now as Thomas urged them to sit and eat with them. He sensed her feelings as the wee lad didn't talk much but watched her with interest.

"I feel bad for him," she said into his mind. *"Losing his mother at three then his dad at five. Being married as a kid then becoming king at such a young age with a false king trying to dethrone and kill him. Nothing like having a target on your back from the get-go."*

"Aye, *things havenae been easy for David,"* he replied. *"But remember if it makes you feel any better, the target is ultimately on the backs of those who are Guardian of this country."*

"Not sure that makes me feel any better," she said. *"Thomas seems nice."*

"Aye," he returned. *"Unfortunately, nice people die far too often around here."*

"No doubt." Her eyes met his as she sipped wine. *"I'm sensing you're running a little grumpy."*

"Aren't you?" He swigged his whisky. *"'Tis not easy finally having you only to not really have you."*

"Technically, you did, though," she reminded. *"The deed's done."*

Truly? She had never uttered more untrue words.

"The deed? Done?" he exclaimed. *"We were nowhere near finished, and that wasnae a deed by any means but a tease."*

Her cheeks flushed. *"A tease that felt damn good."*

"Aye," he agreed, looking at her with promise, eager to taste her sweet juices again. Eager to see her fulfilled in every way imaginable. *"But not nearly as good as 'twill feel once I've had ye as ye should be had. Pleased as ye should be pleased. Fulfilled in every sense of the word."*

A becoming pink stained her cheeks and highlighted her freckles.

"'Tis good to know ye will be staying on with us," Thomas said, pulling them back into a conversation the man had no idea they'd detoured from. "Bravery such as yers is welcome indeed, lass."

Interestingly, only Tiernan and Julie had witnessed the blade running through her. To everyone else's eyes, including Aidan's, she had simply twirled David away before the blade had a chance to find its mark.

If only it had been that simple.

While beyond relieved that Julie had lived, he wasn't sure he would ever get over seeing her like that. Feeling her life seep away. Knowing he was losing her. Though he had suffered his fair share of loss, the sensation had been the first of its kind. Crippling in how it seemed to suck the life from him. Now he knew with certainty he would only be a husk of a man if he lost her because she would take his soul with her.

When her eyes met his, he realized she was following his every thought.

More so, that she felt the same.

"We wouldn't be anywhere else," she replied to Thomas then smiled warmly at David again. "It's our pleasure and honor."

Not for the first time, he saw a flicker of genuine affection in the lad's eyes as he looked at her. She was good with kids. That was clear. For reasons they both understood, he had avoided outright asking her if she wanted children of her own. Yet there was no need to ask anymore. He saw it in the way she looked at David. In the thoughts that warmed her heart.

"You want them too," she murmured into his mind, stating rather than asking. She met his eyes. *"You could have had them by now. Should have."*

"As could you have."

"Not with my house-hopping lifestyle."

"Of course you could," he returned. *"You were just waiting for the right man and the right bairns."*

"There are right children?"

"Aye," he confirmed. *"The wee bairns meant for you come from me...from us."*

"You waited, too, didn't you?" Her internal voice was soft, curious. *"You waited for me even though you knew we couldn't be together?"*

117

"I knew no such thing," he replied. *"If I havenae made that clear by now, I will gladly spend the rest of my life convincing you."*

She was about to reply but got distracted by something unseen. Something she sensed. For a split second, he swore her ring flickered with magic before her attention turned to David. What was that all about? Because whatever it was had to do with the king. He was sure of it.

"You were very brave today, too, King David," she said, a wee touch of awe to her tone when she spoke of David's somewhat odd behavior during battle. "You stood your ground and were very courageous."

"I was?" he asked curiously, at last saying more than a single word at a time. It was clear he thought to correct himself and agree with her because kings were supposed to be courageous, but he instead hesitated, waiting for her answer.

"Yes, I thought you were very courageous, King David." She looked at Thomas and Tiernan. "Don't you agree?"

"Aye," both replied.

In truth, Thomas hadn't been anywhere near David, so he shouldn't be able to say. Tiernan and Aidan had discussed that fact earlier but came to no solid conclusion other than it was odd. Thomas typically stayed close to the wee king, considering himself his main protector.

"Where could he have been?" Julie asked, catching his thoughts.

"He must have been fighting elsewhere," he replied, yet his gut told him that wasn't quite right either. Something had been off. *"Whatever's going on, I think your ring just picked up on it. Your magic."*

"You mean our magic," she replied, relaying what she had just sensed. *"But I agree. Something was off about Thomas not being present, and something was definitely off with David. He seemed out of it, almost."* Her eyes narrowed a little. *"Possessed for lack of a better word."*

A strange sensation washed over him at that.

"Our magic is agreeing with us, Jules."

"I think you're right."

They tried to explore that lead over the next hour or so as they dined with the wee king, but whatever they'd sensed had passed. What had not passed, however, was his growing need for her. Something he made sure she knew the moment they were alone again.

"I should take a bath first," she murmured around kisses, obviously having noted his damp hair earlier. "You clearly had one."

"*Clearly*?" He chuckled. "Not sure if that was a compliment."

"Definitely a compliment." She winked. "But before that, even your stink smelled good."

Thankfully, neither had been overly taxed, so were in the clear, but he looked forward to his magic working as it should again just to be sure. Because, as was the case with all wizards, magic was a handy way to smell better than most who lived in this day and age.

"Are you really worried about bathing?" He murmured a chant out of habit, pleasantly surprised when he managed to remove their shoes and heat the water.

"Oh," she exclaimed, grinning, implying that intimacy might just be their saving grace after all. "Just look at what one good thrust in bed did for you!"

"'Twas a verra good thrust," he conceded.

"Hell yeah, it was." She stepped out of her dress, her smile so wide it warmed his heart. "Who knew one good thrust would make me so happy. Just look what it led to."

He frowned and undressed. "Sexual frustration?"

"No." She stood on her tip-toes and wrapped her arms around his neck. "That thrust proved it's all about the Claddagh ring." She shook her head. "Not the Guardian Witch."

"I suppose it did," he agreed, not about to point out that they didn't know yet if it had affected her magic. "Assuming that thrust caused my magic to start working a wee bit better."

"I'd say it did," she replied, "considering the light sparked in the ring when we were with David so soon afterward."

"So, you saw it shine too?"

He hadn't been sure if she actually saw it or had merely sensed the magic ignite.

"Sure did." She kept grinning. "Which means our magic is growing, not waning." She winked, evidently in an optimistic mood. "Score one for the thrust and lack of virginity I'd say."

"At least for the thrust," he muttered, brushing his lips across hers. "I'll never applaud the lack of virginity."

"You wanted that all for yourself, huh?" she flirted.

"Aye," he sighed, "but 'twas not meant to be."

"Bit of an age difference at the time," she reminded, still grinning. "Besides, you didn't save yours for me."

"Trust me, that's probably a good thing." He swept her up then sat her down in the tub. "Better that I had some experience first, aye?"

"Oh, I don't know." She admired his cock and licked her lips. "I think I would have enjoyed teaching you a thing or two." She gripped it. "Making you all mine."

Before he knew it, she truly was making him all hers when she came up and took him into her mouth. Yet another fantasy that fell short of the real thing.

"Bloody hell," he rasped, realizing quickly that she was talented at this. So good that he could barely keep his eyes open to watch her. And watching truly was a pleasure. By the time she finished, he could barely stand, he released so hard. A release she saw through to the very end, enjoying all he had to give.

"There." She licked her lips again and laid back. "I've wanted to do that for a while."

"And I've wanted you to do that for a while." He grabbed a washcloth and crouched beside her. "I've wanted to do a lot of things."

"Like have kids," Julie said softly. She went to take the cloth from him, but he shook his head, intending to wash her himself.

He was glad she wanted to talk about this again so soon. "Aye, like kids."

"I'm not on the pill, Tiernan." Her guilty eyes met his. "Sorry, I should've told you sooner, especially considering your magic's haywire." She shook her head. "It was irresponsible of me."

He ran the cloth over her back. "Why?"

"Uh, because you could've got me pregnant with that one thrust." She frowned. "Not to mention, what if I were wrong when I said we should go for it and have sex? What if it ruined my protective magic, disappointed the Claddagh ring, and proved you were meant for another?" She flinched. "Not good if you got me pregnant."

"Everything's good if I got you pregnant," he countered, ignoring all the rest because none of it mattered. Not when it came to this. "Nothing in all the world in all of the pasts and futures would make me happier, Julie. 'Tis simple as that."

Her eyes lingered on his for a moment before she sank beneath the water then surfaced. She never did respond to his statement, but he knew how she felt. Relief that he felt the same as her. That she wasn't alone in breaking the rules even when it came to children. That they were, so it seemed, very much in this together at this point, ring confirmation or not. Guardian Witch magic or not. She didn't say anything more as he bathed her, but seemed as lost in the simple act of enjoying each other as he was.

"Tiernan," she eventually began, but he didn't let her get any further because he knew what she wanted. What she needed right now. Had needed since that knock on the door earlier.

So he scooped her up, dried her off then laid her on the bed again. She didn't want foreplay. Just him where he needed to be. Where he was supposed to be. So he spread her thighs and thrust deep only to discover that a single thrust intended to take them even further this time.

-A Scot's Pledge-

Chapter Nineteen

SHE KNEW SOMETHING changed the moment Tiernan thrust, but it didn't matter. All that mattered was this. Him deep inside her. No more interruptions. Just him and her and pure sensation.

Pure love.

Because that's what it was when he finally began moving and sex became so much more than she thought possible. Not just the incredible feeling of him sliding in and out, over and over, but the impact of his gaze on her. The desire and heartfelt emotion simmering in his eyes as they stayed with hers.

She wrapped her legs around him and gripped his forearms, drowning in the feelings he invoked. The fiery passion building between them with every thrust. With every roll of his hips. Sometimes he slowed, others times moved faster, depending it seemed on her expression or the sounds she made.

Enraptured by the way he made her feel, she closed her eyes and pulled him closer still, craving the feel of his slick skin sliding against hers. The moisture dewing between them as their pleasure grew. As they struggled to get closer, deeper.

Fueled by intense passion that only grew stronger, they moved faster until their movements became frenzied and desperate. She raked her nails over his back and ass, hungry for where he was taking her. The steep slope she was climbing. The deep dive she would be taking over the edge.

One that came so hard and so fast, she flew over it before she knew what hit her.

She cried out, vaguely aware that he had followed. Vaguely aware that he had pressed deep and throbbed inside her. That he thrust his hips ever-so-slowly still, staying deep, draining himself against her womb.

"I love you, Tiernan," she whispered, finally feeling like she could say it out loud. That caring for him couldn't be snatched away from her.

"I know, lass," he murmured in her ear. "But 'tis nice to finally hear aloud."

"It is, isn't it?" she said softly, finally opening her eyes only to realize they weren't where they were supposed to be. The bed and ceiling were gone. Instead, she lay on grass with nothing but the night sky overhead. "Oh, my God!"

"Och," he muttered, rolling off her. Thankfully, he was able to chant clothes on them without a problem. "We're back at the *Fir bhrèige.*"

"This is good," she murmured, convinced of it. She eyed the silent sentinels surrounding them. Fog drifted in heavy swirls around the monoliths. "I told you we needed to return to the Calanais Standing Stones, and here we are." She met his eyes. "Here we are after being intimate, with your magic seemingly on track again."

"Intimate in the heart of stones that have witnessed great magic, both light and dark." He helped her up. "I dinnae know if that is good or not. How dangerous it might be."

When she frowned in question, he went on. "Whilst 'tis clear it helped us, it may have also made us vulnerable to whatever dark magic was here."

"So sort of like what happened at the stones in Ireland?"

"Aye, somewhat." He shook his head. "Even now, I cannae pinpoint precisely where the dark magic emanates from." His gaze went to the tomb. "Though 'tis strongest there."

She started for the tomb, curious if her newfound magic might help her discover more, but he grabbed her wrist and shook his head. "Nay, dinnae go near it right now."

She started to respond but sensed something moments before she heard a strange sound.

"Did you hear that?" she whispered.

"Aye." He pulled her close and narrowed his eyes at the ever-thickening fog drifts. "'Tis within the fog…or beyond it, further out."

"It's a woman's voice." She tilted her head and listened. "I think."

"Aye, 'tis," he said. "'Tis a lass, and she's coming closer."

"She is…" Julie agreed. "From that direction." She drifted toward one of the stones, still straining to hear. "She's talking to someone, but I don't hear anyone responding." Seconds later, the voice became clear. "Oh, shit, it's Chloe!"

She raced to the stone with Tiernan right behind her, but there was nobody there.

"I hear her clear as day though!" She walked around the stone, inspecting it. "Right here."

"No, right here," Chloe exclaimed, appearing on the other side of the rock. "What on Earth is going on?"

"Chloe!" She embraced her friend then held her at arm's length. "Are you okay? How did you get here?"

"Where *is* here?" Chloe said slowly, looking Julie over. "And what are you wearing?"

Rather than wait for a response, her friend eyed the tall standing stone next to her with curiosity rather than fear like anyone in their right mind would. Because she most certainly wasn't where she had been a moment before, and that should scare the hell out of her.

But that was Chloe. Curious to a fault. Always looking for her next scoop.

"One second I was exploring the Stonehenge," Chloe went on, "then a woman appeared out of nowhere." She frowned, considering that. "I can't quite recall what we talked about." Her eyes widened. "But I *do* remember hearing a guy with a Scottish brogue on the other side of the rock I was standing beside. He was calling out for…" She looked skyward, trying to remember before her eyes widened. "Maeve! That was it." She nodded once, sure of it. "Her name was Maeve."

Julie and Tiernan frowned at each other before something occurred to her, and she looked at Chloe again. "Did the man sound like Tiernan?"

"Yeah, very similar, actually." Chloe considered him for a moment. "Not sure the voice was exactly the same, though."

"You think it was Aidan, aye?" Tiernan said into Julie's mind. *"That somehow his dream at the stones in Ireland is connected to this?"*

"He did hear Maeve on the other side," she reminded. *"As well as another woman's voice he didn't recognize."*

"What did he say?" Tiernan asked Chloe.

"Um…" She pondered it absently, still inspecting the rock. "He was telling Maeve he was there. To come to him." Her brows drew together as she ran her fingers over the stone. "You know now that I think about it, he sounded desperate and sad." She frowned and looked at them. "Why was he so sad?" Her voice dropped to a whisper, her words unexpected as she seemed to answer her own question. "Because he won't be separated from her forever…He'll find her again."

"Maeve?" Julie asked softly, truly wowed by all this.

"Yeah…I think…" Chloe frowned again and shook her head. "Or maybe not." She blinked a few times and focused on them, finally realizing how out of whack things really were. That she wasn't where she was supposed to be. "Where the hell *am* I?"

"I think the ring is making all of this easier for her," Tiernan explained. *"Or her initial reaction would have been stronger."*

"Maybe," Julie agreed. *"But then this is Chloe. Her curiosity could walk her right off a cliff, and she wouldn't realize it until it was too late."* She sighed. *"Now, to figure out how to drop the bombshell that she fell through time instead."*

"'Tis best to share things in small bits," he advised. *"Let her ease into the bigger picture?"*

"Ease into the bigger picture?" She glanced at him, amused. *"Is that what I've been doing?"*

"Nay, you've been part of the bigger picture from the verra beginning," he replied. *"You just didnae know it yet."*

They both started at his words, recognizing that he wasn't just saying that because he wished it but voiced what their magic told him to. The truth they could see clearly now that they'd been intimate.

"It turns out you're on a bit of an adventure," she said to Chloe, focusing on her friend when she was super eager to discover what other truths might be revealed about her own role in all this. "You've sort of…" How to phrase this? *Come on, Julie. You're used to dealing with time travelers.* Not like this, though. "Well...have you ever watched Dr. Who?"

"Can't say I have." Chloe's eyes remained narrowed as she tried to figure everything out. "I've heard of it though...time travel show, right?"

"Yup." She was about to say more when Chloe shook her head and blinked several times again.

"Wait...right...." Chloe peered at her ring, understanding dawning out of nowhere. "Time travel...this." Her eyes shot to Tiernan, taking in his medieval attire before she did the same to Julie and whispered, "Holy hell, the dream..."

"You said the magic of the ring is easing her into things," she said into Tiernan's mind. *"But is it safe to say whatever Adlin and likely Grant did to it beforehand is affecting her transition too?"*

"Aye, I'd say so," he replied. *"At least in part."*

"In part?"

"Aye, 'tis hard to know what else might be influencing her," he said. *"Mayhap the stones or even more likely, the MacLomain she's destined for."*

"Or Hamilton," she murmured, referring to Aidan.

"Or Hamilton," he concurred.

"What dream, Chloe?" she said aloud. Her friend was back to gazing around.

Chloe's eyes grew more concerned by the moment, the dream evidently not a top priority anymore.

"I need to find him," Chloe said more to herself than them. "I think I have a message for him."

"A message for who, lass?" Tiernan said.

"Him." Chloe's suddenly haunted eyes met his. "The guy on the other side of the stone."

"You sound like you know him," Julie said.

"I just need to find him," Chloe kept saying, turning again and again, looking from stone to stone. "He's just on the other side...I know he is."

Tiernan and Julie glanced at each other in confusion and concern moments before Chloe locked onto the stone next to the one she had appeared at and strode that way.

"Chloe, stop!" Julie pursued her, but it was too late.

Her friend had vanished.

Stranger still, seconds later, someone else appeared in the very same spot.

Chapter Twenty

"BLOODY HELL," AIDAN exclaimed, appearing where Chloe had stood moments before. "Am I still dreaming?"

"I dinnae think so," Tiernan replied, as curious as Julie about what was happening. "What do you last remember, Cousin?"

"Drifting off to sleep," Aidan exclaimed, "at the king's holding." He shook his head. "Then I was dreaming about the Stonehenge in New Hampshire. There was a woman there. I couldnae see her, but..." He paused, the curious look on his face nearly identical to the one Chloe had just worn. "She was trying to tell me something." He nodded once, sure of it. "She had a message for me." He gazed around. "Then I was at another Stonehenge before I ended up here."

"What Stonehenge?"

"I dinnae know with certainty because there was so much fog."

"There was here too," Julie murmured. "Now it's gone. Just like Chloe."

"Chloe?" Aidan looked at them in confusion. "Why does that name sound familiar?"

"My guess?" Tiernan said. "Because you dreamt of her though you've never actually met."

He filled his cousin in on everything that had happened.

"She mentioned Maeve?" Aidan said softly. "Truly?"

"Yeah." Julie eyed him. "When you had that dream about the stones in Ireland, did you call out to Maeve? Did you ask her to come to you?"

"I might have called out to her." He shook his head. "But I'm certain I didnae tell her to come to me."

Tiernan and Julie glanced at each other again, of the same mind.

"I think we should tread verra carefully when it comes to those we see or hear beyond Brouns in our dreams." Tiernan gestured at the Stonehenge. "Especially at any of these locations, past or present."

Aidan considered him, catching on fast.

"You think though I called for Maeve, one of the warrior monks was using my voice to summon Chloe somehow," he surmised. "That her curiosity would draw her though 'twas not her name."

Julie glanced at Aidan with surprise. "How do you know Chloe's that curious?"

He shook his head, troubled. "I dinnae know. Am I right?"

"Yes."

"'Tis hard to know what happened to you at those stones in Ireland, Aidan," Tiernan went on, staying focused. "But something doesnae feel right about it." He cocked his head. "You were pinned to the stone in your dream, right?"

"Aye." Aidan nodded. "'Twas alarming."

"No doubt." Tiernan pondered that. "You said something came in your dream, Cousin. Something dark. Might it have been the warrior monks' magic at work? Or should I say, did it feel like verra ancient, powerful magic? A sorcery unknown to us?"

"Not warrior monks but the disinherited," Julie corrected. The stone in her ring flared to life. "That's what they should be called because that's what they are."

Tiernan looked from her to the ring and nodded. She was right. Their magic had just confirmed it.

"I couldnae tell much other than something dark was closing in," Aidan supplied, disgruntled. "I might have sensed more if my magic wasnae so off."

"Yet it *was* dark magic," Tiernan said softly, feeling the magic of Julie's Claddagh ring. Hearing its message. "'Twas the same power that was in the woodland yesterday when we were attacked." He looked at Julie. "'Twas also around wee David…"

"Possessing him," she whispered, then shook her head, speaking about what the ring's magic had been trying to convey when they dined with David earlier. Something they had tried to figure out then set aside when they became intimate. "No, not possessing *him* but those around him." She frowned. "Not to say whatever it was didn't have David cast beneath some sort of spell because he certainly wasn't himself."

"Nay." He was more concerned by what he suddenly knew with certainty when a blocked memory came rushing back. "That was one of his own guardsmen that turned on him, wasn't it?" It was so clear now. "The one I killed after I thought you were stabbed."

"Yeah, pretty sure it was." She narrowed her eyes. "But how is that possible? Others had to have seen him. It would have been talked about. They would have looked for more traitors, right?"

"If, in fact, that man had been seen for who he really was," Aidan said. "Which I can assure you he wasnae because I clearly saw a rebel clansman as did the others."

"A rebel clansman," Tiernan repeated, thinking it over. "What were his tartan colors?"

Aidan frowned. "Come to think of it I didnae see any colors."

"Then how can you be sure he was Scottish?"

"Because he was dressed like a Scotsman," Aidan began then frowned and blinked as though realizing something. "Which, in retrospect, doesnae mean he was Scottish." He shook his head. "Yet he verra much struck me and everyone who fought on behalf of wee King David as one of our countrymen."

"Which would be pretty clever of the Disinherited if they wanted to continue causing dissent among their enemies," Julie pointed out. "More than that, if they wanted to show others how much unrest the country suffered under its current leadership."

Tiernan crossed his arms over his chest. "So, you think they were pretenders?"

"Why not?"

"Why not indeed," he murmured. "Grant said he had sensed one of the nobles had changed but wasn't sure how. Mayhap 'twas specifically his influence in the woodland."

"Without a doubt," came a familiar voice before Grant appeared.

This time he appeared older, his hair sprinkled with white. He muttered something about quite enjoying his younger self again but that his ethereal form was like ashes on the wind lately. "'Tis as we suspected. The nobles, or should I say whatever is manipulating them, are accessing ley-lines that should not be theirs to access."

"That's why the lines looked different," Julie whispered. "Darker." She was putting the pieces together. "They're definitely using some of them to travel like I do...not that I know exactly how I do that yet."

"Aye, they're using them for just that, lass," Grant confirmed, grim. "And they first accessed them here at these stones." He homed in on the rock behind Aidan then looked at him in surprise. "It brought you here then?"

"So it seems," he replied. "In a dream against my will at that."

"Och, nay, this was not against your will, lad." Grant looked from Julie to Aidan. "This was with aid from Julie's inner Guardian Witch, trying to bridge the gap betwixt you and your Broun."

"Chloe, then?" Julie said.

"Aye, I would say so." Grant grinned at Aidan. "I've seen her in my travels, you know. She's a verra fetching lass."

Aidan crossed his arms over his chest as though fending off a possible romance but nodded graciously because he would always put duty to clan and country first.

"You'll see," Grant assured. "She'll likely keep you on your toes, too. Which will eventually appeal to the strict moral boundaries you've created for your heart and soul."

"I didnae do that." Aidan cocked his head, perplexed. "And if I did, why would such a lass appeal to me?"

"'Tis always exciting to be freed of your boundaries, lad," Grant scoffed before he waved it away and focused on more pressing matters. He looked at Julie and Tiernan. "Tell me, when you traveled back to the era when these stones were resurrected and witnessed the Guardian Witch ceremony, would you say that the sun setting on the solstice was the initial source of power? That which led to the creation of the ring?"

"Undoubtedly," they confirmed at the same time.

"Aye, then," Grant replied. "'Tis important that."

"Why?"

"Because 'tis a doorway directly linked to your magic, Julie," he revealed. "One that can be opened and closed by you." He looked to where Tiernan's tattoo was located, clearly aware it was there. "And mayhap he who you protect." He gave them a telling look. "I believe you have the power to seal the enemy's magic out of at least these stones. This Stonehenge." His gaze flickered over where they had been lying on the grass before his amused eyes returned to them. "In fact, I'd hazard to say you've already started the process."

Julie's mouth fell open then snapped shut before she spoke into Tiernan's mind. *"Please tell me he's not referring to us having sex."*

"Aye, 'twas the intimacy." Grant grinned, catching their internal conversation. "And 'tis bloody good I caught that thought." He looked between the men. "That means that though 'tis only a wee bit right now, MacLomain magic is starting to stabilize."

"I think mine is beginning to return," Tiernan informed. "'Tis not one hundred percent but far better." He looked at her ring. "Not to mention the stone is starting to shine."

"A stone that originally came from this verra Stonehenge." Grant nodded, pleased. "I must be off to confer with Adlin about this." His gaze went from the ring to Tiernan's tattoo then he looked to the sky though he could not see the ley-lines. "Keep an eye to the things that guide your way."

"Wait," Tiernan said before Grant could whisk away. "What were you going to say about the solstice? How are Julie and I supposed to close the gateway? When we do, will it end whatever's affecting everyone's magic? Mayhap cripple the Disinherited?"

"Och, nay, if only it were that simple." Grant sighed. "From what I'm sensing, 'twill simply seal this particular Stonehenge, which in turn will help you against the threat rising up." He looked between the three of them with a grave expression. "Make no mistake, this is but the beginning of us defeating monsters that have been around as long as Guardian Witches if not longer."

"Who are they?" Tiernan asked.

"I havenae figured that out yet," Grant replied. "But Julie is right about them being called the Disinherited. Because whatever injustice they felt they suffered aligns with the noblemen determined to own Scotland one way or another." When he shook his head, his body caught on the wind for a moment before it straightened again. "Whoever they are, they siphoned the magic of the Guardian Witches' power in this place, then morphed and twisted it with their own magic. That is why they can use the ley-lines."

He looked into the distance as though seeing another Stonehenge though it was halfway across Scotland. "Their magic is attached to all the Stonehenges I mentioned and in turn, not just Julie, but he who she protects. A MacLomain. Then through him, his kin." He looked southwest as though gazing across the Atlantic itself. "Through them, the Brouns and their Stonehenge."

"My God," Julie exclaimed. "My friends are really vulnerable then." She shook her head. "I've got to find a way back, seeing how the ley-lines don't seem to be getting me there."

"They may not be getting you there in an obvious way," Grant replied. "But understand this, lass. Dark magic might have taken advantage of Guardian Witch magic, but it works in reverse too. In a way, especially as you grow stronger, your magic protecting the MacLomains protects their true loves as well." He gave her a compassionate look. "I know this is difficult for you to grasp and frustrating because you cannae control it yet, or even ever entirely, but 'tis magic not necessarily meant to be completely controlled. Not by your mind anyway."

"Then, by what?"

"Your heart," he said softly, looking between them. "Don't you see? The more you accept what you feel is yours and always has been, the more love you provide your magic. That, in turn, will start a chain that follows your magic and ley-lines. Then it will help spark that very love in others." His knowing gaze drifted to Aidan. "Dormant love just waiting to connect with its other half."

Chapter Twenty-One

"I GUESS IT'S a good thing I love you." She grinned at Tiernan. "Or all this might've gone to hell."

"It still might," Aidan reminded. "If we dinnae get back to the wee king."

"Very true." She shook her head. "Grant might have shared all sorts of new things, yet I feel like he left us with more questions than answers."

"Aye." Tiernan sighed. "Like da, that tends to be his way. Especially when he's unraveling a mystical puzzle."

Grant had poofed away a few minutes ago, his departing words only that they best be off in the direction meant for them.

"Why didn't he just say back to David?"

"Because he's taken on Adlin's cryptic tendencies," Aidan muttered, studying the stone he had appeared in front of.

"Or mayhap he's quite literal." Tiernan looked to the ley-lines he could evidently see again no doubt because they'd been intimate. "'Tis your magic we must follow, lass." He shrugged a shoulder. "Mayhap 'tis not supposed to bring us back to the king quite yet."

"*Our* magic," she corrected then considered the lines too. "How am I supposed to sense where to go if I have no idea where that might be other than back to David?"

"I think if you keep in mind that you need to protect the king," he replied, "then it will take us where we are supposed to go. 'Twill show us the next leg of our journey. One that will ultimately keep him safe."

"Sounds reasonable." She sighed and mulled over her surroundings. "And exactly how do I do that again?"

Tiernan pulled her into his arms. "For starters, your magic seems at its best when we're close." He tilted her chin up and brushed his lips across hers. "When you're not giving things too much thought but giving yourself over to something else."

"Something else?" she mused. "Don't you mean *someone* else?"

"Aye," he murmured. "Me."

He kissed her again, this time more passionately, and proved he was right.

Bright light flashed, and they found themselves…right where they had started.

"'Tis daytime now," Aidan said, pointing out the obvious, clearly glad to be along. "Yet, we didnae travel."

"Not from our location," Tiernan agreed. "But mayhap to a different era."

"The stones look the same," she pointed out. "So it wasn't way back in time again, at least."

"Nay." Aidan's gaze narrowed on the horizon. "So, what's next?"

"I have no idea." She frowned and looked around. Her ring wasn't shining, so no help there. Then she remembered what Grant had said and looked at Tiernan's shoulder. Evidently of the same mind, he was already pulling up his sleeve.

"Whoa," she whispered when he revealed it. "Do you see that?"

"Aye," he said. "'Tis a bluish-green line running from the center to the outer edge."

"A ley-line," she whispered. "It's not pointing at one of the four stones in the tattoo but sort of in between."

Aidan joined them and peered at it before he looked in the direction the line was pointing. "Mayhap 'tis telling you where we need to go next."

They looked at him, surprised.

"You can see it too?" Julie asked.

"Aye," Aidan replied.

She looked up. "What about lines in the sky?"

He shook his head. "Nay."

"Interesting." She met Tiernan's eyes. "What do you make of that?"

"I dinnae know, but I'd say Aidan seeing the line on my tattoo is a step in the right direction." He eyed the line then looked where it led. "You're right about it pointing out which way we should go, Aidan. I'm sure of it."

She perked her brows at Tiernan. "So essentially your tat's a magical compass?"

"I'd say so." He kept looking in that direction. "We willnae know for sure though until we head that way and see if it leads us where we're meant to go."

"Very true."

So they headed in that direction only for everything to transform the moment they stepped beyond the stones.

"What the…" She spun only to find the Stonehenge vanished and the landscape entirely different. "What happened? Where are we?"

Tiernan's gaze swept over their surroundings before he looked at Aidan. "We're near the east coast now, aye? It looks like an area north of East Lothian."

"Aye, 'tis," Aidan confirmed. "We've been shifted clear across Scotland." His gaze turned west. "And we're not alone."

"Och," Tiernan muttered, pulling her after him. "Those are Sassenach soldiers. We need to find woodland and hide until we know what's going on."

Thankfully, the forest wasn't too far off, and they made it undetected.

"There are caves in this direction." Tiernan led them deeper into the forest. Late day sun cut through the trees, and a blustery wind blew. "'Twill keep us out of sight until we figure out our next move."

"What time period do you think this is?" she asked. "Yours, maybe?"

"'Tis impossible to know," Tiernan said. "Though 'twas spring there and 'tis clearly summer here."

He was right. The season had changed. But that didn't mean the year had.

"In here." He led them into a small cave behind a thick wall of shrubbery. "We'll give it a wee bit o' time, then I'll scout."

"Nay, I'll scout," Aidan said. "'Tis best you stay with Julie and protect her."

She looked at Tiernan's shoulder. "Is the line still on your tat?"

When he lifted his sleeve, it was gone.

"It'll be back," she murmured, convinced of it as she ran her fingers around the circle. "I just know it."

He nodded in agreement, clearly sensing the same.

Aidan ended up waiting an hour to confirm they hadn't been followed before he left, and Tiernan felt it safe enough to start a fire. It might be summer, but the wind was chilly and the cave even chillier.

Once the fire was crackling, he sat on a rock and plunked her down on his lap. It seemed English soldiers had swiftly become the last thing on his mind, which suited her just fine.

She grinned. "I can just as easily sit on my own rock."

"I *am* your rock." He fingered a curl affectionately and met her eyes. "Do you know how many times I envisioned pulling you onto my lap? Talking to you this way rather than you sitting elsewhere?"

"No," she murmured.

He slowly wrapped the curl around his finger. "And you cannae imagine how many times I wanted to play with these curls, and run my fingers through them."

"Not always the easiest thing to do with my hair." She traced the tip of her finger along his strong jaw. "And I wanted to do this." She touched the corner of his mouth. "Sometimes, I wanted to pretend you had food on the corner of your mouth so I could touch here."

"I wish you had," he murmured and kissed her finger. "I wish we had just done the things we wanted to do."

"But we couldn't," she whispered. "Not then."

"Nay, not then, but we can now." He traced his fingers over her shoulder blade and brushed back her unruly curls. "I wanted to do this when we sat beneath the old oak, not just so I could touch your hair but feel the warmth of your skin through your shirt. So I could see the way the sun speckled your neck on a warm summer day."

She tugged gently at his shirt. "And God knows, I wanted you to finally take your damn shirt off on a warm summer day."

He grinned and pulled it off now. In turn, she lowered the corner of her dress, giving him full access to her shoulder.

"Och, if I'd seen this then," he kissed it softly, "I would have wanted to do that."

Just the feel of his warm lips brushing her skin made her breath catch and her nerve endings come alive. "If you'd done that, I would have wanted to do this." She cupped his cheek. "Touching you like this while looking into your eyes." It was hard to find her voice as emotions bubbled up, so she whispered, "I always loved your eyes. Especially when they looked my way."

"And they always did," he murmured, reminding her of how his magic first sparked. "From the verra beginning."

As she gazed into his eyes, remembering all the times, all the ages, that moment came rushing back. When his magic first flared.

"I saw it then," she whispered, startled, her magic evidently unlocking a memory. "For just a flicker of a moment."

"What, lass?"

"This." She brushed her fingers over his tattoo. "For a split second, it was there before your magic flared…or maybe it was within your magic." She shook her head. "How could I have forgotten I saw that shape? It almost seemed forged within your very magic…part of it somehow."

"Because this represents the stones at the root of your magic," he said softly, referring to the tattoo. "And I am the one you are meant to protect." He touched her Claddagh ring. "As I am meant to protect you."

Before she could respond, his lips were on hers, and she was more than ready. They had a lot of lost time to make up for. Especially him considering he had lived far more life since they met.

He dug his fingers into her hair as the kiss deepened.

"Yet another thing I wanted to do," he murmured into her mind. *"As you can imagine, I was often in a verra difficult state by the time I left you."*

"I wasn't much better off." She rubbed herself back and forth along his erection, so turned on it hurt. *"I used to imagine what it would've been like if you showed up in the shower…or maybe when I was doing something naughty to myself."*

He growled into her mouth and hoisted her until she straddled him.

"What are you doing," she half gasped, half groaned. "Aidan could return at any second…or an English soldier could show up!"

"I will know if anyone's close." He adjusted her dress and panties until the throbbing flesh between her thighs was against him, yet her skirt covered everything else.

"But is your magic a sure thing right now?" she murmured, her voice raspy with desire, her concern over being caught by his cousin or discovered by the enemy fading fast.

"Aye, my magic is sure enough." He freed himself and grabbed her ass over her skirt, steering her where he wanted her. "If not, I'll hear them coming."

"They might be light on their feet," was all she got out before he drove himself deep inside.

"I cannae tell ye how many times I wanted to do that, lass," he groaned, his brogue as thick as the masterpiece between his legs.

"Tell me more," she half whispered, half whimpered, liking where this was going in more ways than one. "Tell me what you wanted to do to me."

"We would have been sitting on that old swing hanging from the oak in front of the colonial in New Hampshire," he said, not moving, driving her crazy with anticipation.

"That would've been a trick," she managed. Taking the initiative, she rolled her hips, enjoying the way his muscles tensed, and his pupils flared with pent up desire.

"I have excellent balance." He wrapped his hand in her hair again and held tight to her ass with the other. "And strength that would have kept ye right where I wanted ye." He steered her up his shaft so slowly she about came undone. "Ye would have enjoyed the ride from the verra start."

"I bet I would've," she began only to release a strangled cry when he pulled her back down sharply. Sparks of near painful pleasure raced from her womb to every last corner of her body.

"Hell," she gasped, gripping his shoulders when he did it again, and again, over and over. Sometimes torturously slow, other times fast, and hard.

Thankfully, she felt his magic ignite around them so they wouldn't be heard because he definitely made her scream. Something she'd never had a problem with before but couldn't stop now. Not when every move he made, everywhere he touched, made her moan or wail with pleasure.

By the time things got really hot and heavy, she might have even been sobbing it felt so good. When he grabbed her backside with both hands, and she wrapped her arms around him, holding on for dear life, they soared toward a pinnacle that blew her mind when it hit.

He released a strangled groan of pleasure as he thrust deep one last time, held her in place, and exploded inside her. Both trembled, breathing heavily as he held her that way for a time. Eventually, he wrapped his arms around her and held her as tightly as she held him. She could stay in this moment forever it felt so perfect. So meant to be.

Unfortunately, as it turned out, forever would have to wait.

Seconds later, the sound of swords clashing ripped them from bliss.

-A Scot's Pledge-

Chapter Twenty-Two

"STAY HERE, JULIE," he ordered, but naturally, she pursued him, muttering, "Like hell, I will!"

By the time he made it outside, two Sassenach lay slain, and Aidan fought three more.

"Get back inside," he roared into Julie's mind, racing into the fray while simultaneously chanting. Thankfully, his magic downed at least one man, who fell to his knees, gripping his throat as Tiernan's magic strangled him.

That left two.

His cousin crossed blades with one and Tiernan the other, twirling away when the blade swung inches from his face. He spun, ready to counterattack, but magic pulsed out from Julie's ring and flung the man through the air into a tree. Before the warrior slid to the ground, he whipped a dagger and finished him off. Meanwhile, Aidan sliced his blade across his opponent's calf, then spun and drove his sword up under his ribs into his heart.

"Bloody hell," Aidan muttered, wiping away a bit of blood from his lips. "One of them got in a good punch before I downed him."

"I dinnae think I've ever seen you bleed," Tiernan commented. His cousin was a more talented fighter than most and prided himself on finishing his enemies off before they so much as nicked him.

Tiernan headed for Julie and looked her over. "Are you all right?"

"Yes, I'm fine." She cocked her brow, clearly frustrated that he thought to leave her behind yet relieved he was okay. "Your heart might've been in the right place, sweetie, but if I were you, I'd keep your Guardian Witch close." She shook her head. "Not order her to stay behind."

"'Twill take some getting used to," he grumbled then brushed his lips across hers because he couldn't help himself. "But I will try."

"Good." Genuine concern lit her eyes, and she shook her head. "Because I fear for your safety just as much as you do mine."

"Bloody bastard," Aidan muttered, interrupting their conversation. He pulled weapons off the man who had evidently got in the punch. "To hell with ye."

"What happened?" Tiernan asked. "Where did the men come from?"

"'Twas a band split off from the main one we saw." Aidan tossed aside more stolen weapons. As much as they could comfortably carry. "Out to hunt, I'd say, so 'tis only a matter of time before the others realize they arenae coming back." He shook his head. "I only meant to grab one, but the rest saw." He gestured absently in a random direction. "I left one alive to question."

"First, ye've been bloodied." He frowned at Aidan, surprised yet again. "Then seen by the enemy when trying to be stealthy?" He shook his head. "'Tis not like you."

"Nay, 'tis not," Aidan agreed, troubled. "My fluctuating magic is affecting my instincts. My skills as a warrior."

Tiernan knew better than to console him. His cousin had always taken a great deal of pride in his battle skills. Like all things he set his mind to, he'd devoted countless hours fine-tuning his abilities, convinced they would only complement and enhance his powers as a wizard.

Regrettably, it appeared to work both ways.

As it happened, the Sassenach soldier they dragged into the cave to question turned out to be traveling with Balliol and his nobles. So he and Julie's magic had led them in the right direction. Or so they assumed because, according to the man, the year was thirteen thirty-two, and that was relevant.

"So, not all that long after we left David then?" Julie asked after they finished questioning the man.

"Nay." Aidan met Tiernan's eyes. "'Tis the following summer." He shook his head. "Not a good year for our regent."

When Julie looked between them, Tiernan explained.

"Thomas dies this year, lass," he revealed. "Not all that far from this verra location."

"Is David still with him?" She frowned. "He is, right?"

"History is a wee bit fuzzy on that part," Tiernan replied. "Even da and Grant have had issues figuring out exactly what took place."

"Which we can assume has to do with the Disinherited," she said.

"'Twould be my guess," he replied. "Either way, we must return to Thomas and David and remain close to the king. David must survive."

"And Thomas must die," she said softly. "In accordance with history."

"I'm afraid so." He tucked blades here and there on his person. "If he doesnae then things might not go as they should."

"They might go better," she countered.

"'Tis unlikely, lass," Aidan said, strapping on weapons as well. "Especially with dark magic at work."

"Dark magic that has found its way to the twenty-first century," Tiernan added. "Which means not only trouble for Scotland but…"

He trailed off when a strange sensation washed over him.

"But trouble for us too," Julie said, startled as she seemingly sensed the same thing he did. "Or should I say the MacLomain-Broun connection." She frowned at him. "What is this, Tiernan? What am I suddenly feeling?"

"Far more trouble than we anticipated," he murmured, exploring the sensation, the growing certainty. "This is not all about wee David or the Sassenach ruling Scotland but the root of what has saved this country several times over now. That which has kept its history on track."

"Adlin and Iosbail," Julie whispered, exploring the feeling alongside him, understanding more by the moment as her ring ignited. "But of course, it goes back that far."

They weren't talking about his father in this life but the previous. Iosbail had been his foster sister in Ireland and had traveled to Scotland, where she too became immortal, traveling from place to place until she settled in East Lothian.

Until she began the Broun clan.

"That's why we were at the stones in Ireland where da was conceived in that life," Tiernan said. "It went back that far."

"What went back that far?" Aidan asked.

"Injustice," Julie whispered, sensing the darkness that pursued them. Moreover, its possible motive. "Power that should have been theirs..."

"A country that should have been theirs," Tiernan continued, sensing the darkness as well. "The beginning of a verra long vengeance."

"Vengeance born of them being denied," she whispered. "By those who protected...by Guardian Witches." Her eyes sparked with the same light as her ring. "By me and mine." Her voice changed a little, echoing in a way that wasn't quite natural in a cave. "Ready to stand guard once more in the face of fury. In the face of pretenders. Ready to sacrifice to save..."

Whether it was her magic or more, whatever gripped Julie vanished, and she fell to her knees. Fearful, he went to scoop her up, but she shook her head and closed her eyes. "I'm okay." She hung her head. "Just give me a sec."

"What happened?" He crouched in front of her. "What did you just experience?"

"I'm not entirely sure," she whispered, still gathering herself. "I felt like I was here, but not here." She shook her head again. "I've never felt anything like it."

"Were you still in your body?"

"Yes," she said softly before she lifted her head and met his eyes. For a split second, he saw what she'd seen in his eyes when he was an infant. Magic mixed with the design on his shoulder.

Then he felt what she had just felt.

It was almost as though her very soul rushed into him, then bounced back into her body. Then loving warmth poured over him, followed by a fierce need to protect. One, amazingly enough, that far outdid his already overprotective nature.

"It's them," she whispered. "My ancestors...trying to protect your ancestors."

"Aye," he murmured. "Back then and now."

"Happening all at once," she whispered, awed. "Just like your magic saved me when I was stabbed. Magic from the past protecting those in the present. Time folding in on itself giving protective magic the ability to be in two places at once. Giving a single moment the ability to be in two places at once across time."

He was about to add to that, sensing something important, but the fact got away from him before he could voice it. The same thing evidently happened to her because Julie blinked and shook her head. "No, no, no, I almost had it."

"Had what?" Aidan asked as Tiernan helped her to her feet.

"How they're doing it," she murmured. "What my ancestors are trying to tell me."

"Mayhap 'twas all we were supposed to know for now," Tiernan theorized.

"Like dishing out small bits of information at a time to time-travelers." Julie nodded. "You were right."

"So these warrior monks—"

"Disinherited," Julie corrected Aidan.

"The Disinherited," Aidan conceded, going on, "were specifically targeting MacLomains and Brouns before the connection ever even formed betwixt our two clans?"

"MacLomains to be sure," Tiernan said.

"Brouns too." Julie narrowed her eyes. "Just in a different way…for a different purpose."

"What other way could there be than to cease the MacLomain-Broun connection before it has a chance to begin?" Aidan asked. "Do that, and everything that took place over the generations with our kin ceases to exist." His eyes widened a little. "*We* cease to exist."

"Not Julie, though," Tiernan murmured, still trying to grasp what he nearly knew. "She is the one constant in all this." He shook his head. "Even if they destroyed the MacLomains and Brouns at their source, she would still exist."

Or *would* she if Tiernan didn't? *Would* she have existed without he who she protected?

"This is crazy," she whispered, pinching the bridge of her nose. "How am I supposed to fix this when I only get answers in magical bursts of recollection here and there?" Her tired eyes met his. "How am I supposed to save you?" A frown settled on her face. "All of you?"

"With my help." He embraced her, trying to offer comfort. "You need to remember, you're not alone in this, lass. I will always be there with you."

"As will we all if 'tis in our power," Aidan added. "Not only that, but 'tis always best to keep in mind you will get more answers when the time is right." He shook his head. "Dinnae doubt that, lass."

"I wish the time were right now," she murmured, resting her cheek against Tiernan's chest. "If I had the answers up front, it would be so much easier."

"Not necessarily." He stroked her hair. "'Tis hard to know where too much knowledge might lead you. 'Twas done much like this when I helped my Viking ancestors on their quest and 'twas verra much for the best. Time was needed by all to adjust to what had changed. To accept revelations that might have been too much to handle otherwise."

"I hope you're right." She met his eyes again, her gaze a little off. Just like that, her voice was another's and leaden with what he realized was Disinherited possession. "But even if ye are right 'tis too late, wizard. Yer pledge was tested, and ye failed. Now 'tis just a matter of time…"

Chapter Twenty-Three

"I SAID *WHAT?*" she exclaimed. "Seriously?"

"Aye," Aidan confirmed as they made their way into the woodland a short time later. "'Twas all about a pledge made."

"One not seen through." She considered Tiernan. "I know I said it to you, but I get the feeling it was directed at us both. After all, I was supposed to stay in the future to keep an eye on things, and you were supposed to hook up with a Broun to protect your country."

"Which we've established, I'm doing by being with you." He took her hand as they walked. "'Twas but a message designed to spook us." He scowled. "Hopefully, 'twill not happen again." He shook his head. "I dinnae like the Disinherited anywhere near your mind."

"Agreed." She sighed. "So, you think they're just trying to psyche us out?"

"I think that's exactly what they attempted to do," he replied. "The more pressing concern, however, is how they got inside your mind to do so."

"My guess is they somehow slipped in alongside my ancestral message," she said. "If they've found a way to morph the magic from the stones," she tossed him a pointed look of reminder, "stones I'm connected to, then it makes sense they'd be able to slip through when my ancestors are utilizing that magic." She squeezed his hand in reassurance. "The bad guys are gone from my mind now, though. Something you know for certain because you're inside my head far more than they could ever be."

"Aye." Yet his troubled expression remained. "'Tis odd that in possessing you, they didnae possess me."

"Not that odd, really. Not if they were specifically channeling through the Guardian Witch magic." She shook her head. "We might be merging, but your magic is still yours, and mine's still mine." She shrugged. "I just need to learn to control my magic…understand it better."

"Aye," Aidan kicked in. "'Tis likely nothing will be able to get inside you after that because your ancestors' magic will finally be your own."

"It will, won't it?" She stopped short and nodded at Aidan. "That's it." A sense of certainty came over her, and she looked at Tiernan. "That's what it's been all along. My ancestors protecting me from a memory. Better yet whatever my ancestors did to piss off the Disinherited so much, combined with the magic of the past blending with our magic now."

"'Tis all part of your magic sparking," he murmured, sensing it too. "Their magic is streaming through your ring, a natural conduit for MacLomain magic. Protecting you until you can protect yourself."

"Yet, all the while allowing me to protect you." She crossed her arms over her chest. "Which answers a lot but not nearly enough. How am I supposed to seal off the Calanais Stones from the Disinherited? How am I supposed to—"

"You're not supposed to do anything until you know more," Aidan interrupted. "'Twill drive you mad speculating whilst waiting for more truth to be revealed to you."

"Well, that sucks." She scowled and shook her head as they continued on. "It's a damn unsettling feeling not knowing what's next. Not knowing what I'm supposed to do."

"You're supposed to follow the path you're on, Jules," Tiernan said. "To my way of thinking, the fact that the Disinherited felt the need to psyche us out means we're heading in the right direction. That we're truly becoming a threat to whatever their master plan is."

"Good point." She gestured at his shoulder. "That in mind, maybe it's time to check your tat again and make sure we're still walking in the direction it showed us in the cave."

"Aye, 'tis still pointing north," Tiernan confirmed. Moments later, he squinted through the trees. "'Tis on track indeed."

"Where are we," she began only to trail off when something loomed out of the woodland. She sped up a little. "Is that what I think it is?"

"Slow down, lass." Tiernan caught up with her. "Dinnae rush into anything here. Remember that our allies dinnae know if we're friend or foe."

"Right, sorry." She slowed, peering through the trees in awe as they drew closer. "Though it looks a little different, that's Edinburgh Castle, isn't it?"

"'Tis." Tiernan smiled. "Where I imagine we will find wee David."

"There are Scottish soldiers ahead." Aidan glanced at Tiernan. "You stay here. I'll—"

"Nay, not with your magic so off." He shook his head. "We go on together."

"Aye, then."

"We are friends of the rightful king, David II," Tiernan called out when they were close enough that the soldiers could hear them. "We come with news for Regent Sir Thomas Randolph."

As it turned out, they ran into very little trouble when the men saw Tiernan's tartan colors.

"So Thomas kept his men on alert for your return?" she asked.

They broke the wood line, and she finally saw the castle in all its glory. Its battlements stood tall against the setting sun. She had visited this castle in the twenty-first century, so it was pretty mind-blowing seeing it now. Gone were the tourists with their cell phone cameras. Instead, people in medieval clothing sold wares from carts, and well-armed men rode by on horses. The air smelled of torch smoke and a variety of other aromas, some more pungent than others.

The yellow and red lion rampant flag flew proudly, reminding her that Scotland's modern-day sky blue flag with its white saltire cross wouldn't come into existence until around fifteen thirteen. Not for another hundred and eighty-one years. It also reminded her that someday the English flag would fly one turret higher than the Scottish on this very castle.

"Aye, Thomas has kept an eye out for our return," Tiernan said in answer to her question, pulling her from her reverie. He put a hand to the small of her back as they made their way through the crowd.

"My parents and aunts and uncles had the same advantage with Sir William Wallace and King Robert the Bruce on their adventures."

"Handy," she murmured, enraptured by the fortress-like castle on the cliff as they approached. "Good to know Thomas is still around too and not…"

She trailed off, not particularly wanting to think about the man's unfortunate future.

As they soon learned, the regent was well aware that Balliol's men were gathering in the south to fight.

"By the bloody rood," Thomas muttered a short time later, "he's a pain in my arse."

They strode down a hallway she hadn't seen in the twenty-first century. But then parts of the castle had been knocked down several times over the centuries either in battle or intentionally to dissuade the enemy from desiring it.

"Him and the bloody nobles," Thomas went on. "Traitorous countrymen, all!"

"What do ye intend to do?" Tiernan asked. They entered a dining area free of people where Thomas urged them to sit. "Stand yer ground here or go fight him?"

"Go fight him to be sure." Thomas continued muttering under his breath about traitors as food and drink were served. "I've enough men. There's no need to suffer a long, expensive siege."

"Isn't it safer to stay near the king, though?" Julie asked. "Why not stay here and fight outside the gates if need be?"

He frowned at her then gave Tiernan a look she wanted to wipe off his face.

"'Tis a sad day when a MacLomain lets his lass speak so boldly." Thomas' brows whipped together. "Especially when a lass should have no say in matters such as this." His eyes narrowed on her. "'Tis clear enough she's from these parts and should know better."

"*Excuse* me," Julie began but snapped her mouth shut when Tiernan shot her a look.

"I apologize, Regent," Tiernan said dutifully. "'Twill not happen again."

Before she could speak, he spoke in her mind. *"Something is off with him, Julie. Set aside your anger and help me figure out what that is."* He looked at her and spoke aloud. "If ye hope to remain by my side ye best watch yer tongue, lass."

This was going to take some patience, wasn't it? Yet when she caught little David out of the corner of her eye peeking around the corner, she did what she needed to do.

"Of course," she murmured softly, lowering her head subserviently. "I am sorry."

Thomas didn't bother with a response but continued sharing his battle strategy, which, as far as she could tell, pretty much stunk.

"So what are we thinking?" she said into Tiernan's mind. *"That a Disinherited is possessing him?"*

"'Tis quite possible," he replied. *"Though you would think if that were the case, he would just do away with David now. He has easy enough access."*

"True." She offered a small smile hello but little more when David peeked around the corner again. Best to keep Thomas' attention off the boy. *"I'd nearly forgotten that Thomas heard my voice as though I'm from here. Any new thoughts about that?"*

"Only that you're meant to be here," came Aidan's voice in their minds. Though tempted to glance at him in surprise because he'd not only heard their internal conversation but spoke telepathically, they remained focused on Thomas.

"You're speaking in our minds, Cousin," Tiernan remarked. *"That's a good sign."*

"Aye," Aidan agreed. *"Verra."*

If he spoke after that, they didn't hear him, so they questioned him later after leaving Thomas' company. The regent had continued to treat her far differently than he had at the beginning, his regard for women callous.

"What happened back there, Aidan?" Tiernan asked. The three of them sat in front of a fire in one of the chambers they had been given for the night. "You mentioned that Julie's accent sounded correct to Thomas because she was meant to be here, then you went silent."

"Actually, I continued talking, but you never responded," Aiden revealed. "I saw a flash of the Stonehenge in Ireland and knew for certain she was supposed to be here. So much so that her magic will do whatever it takes to ensure that. To see things through."

She narrowed her eyes. "What does Thomas hearing a local accent have to do with me seeing things through?"

"I dinnae know," Aidan replied. "All I know is what I told you. 'Tis interesting that it happened right before your mind opened to mine, aye? As though 'twas intentional."

"You think 'twas her ancestors sending her a message?" Tiernan said.

"Aye, to be sure." Aidan wore a thoughtful expression. "But more than that too...a bridge of sorts struggling to connect a divide."

"What does that mean?" she asked. "Like your magic getting back to what it should be?"

"In part," Aidan said. "'Tis verra hard to describe but most welcome. Whatever it is, it means to connect those it wishes to protect."

"Like MacLomains with fellow MacLomains not to mention MacLomains with Brouns?" She shook her head and glanced at Tiernan. "Though I thought that happened all on its own anyway."

"It typically does," he replied. "As they grow closer." He looked at Aidan. "What you're implying sounds like it's happening beyond the normal MacLomain-Broun true love connection."

"Mayhap," Aidan said softly. "But why would that be? Telepathically connecting was always a telling part of MacLomains and Brouns coming together. It allowed them to know they were with the right person, did it not?"

"Aye," Tiernan concurred. "But then their magic wasnae fluctuating. Their clansmen werenae forgetting MacLomains ever had magic." His gaze went to Julie. "And they didnae have a Guardian Witch thrown into the mix to protect them. One who I know will keep us on course."

"While I'm glad I've got your vote," she sighed and sipped her whisky, "I'm not so sure you should be singing my praises quite yet."

"Too late." Aidan shrugged. "Besides, you always put Tiernan first and saved our good king. How can I not sing praises for such a lass?"

"Well, I appreciate your vote of confidence." She toasted him. "Here's hoping when push comes to shove I don't let you down."

"You will," Tiernan whispered. She felt the strange sensation that washed over him when he looked at her with suddenly haunted eyes. "You willnae disappoint me...but ye will verra much disappoint someone."

Chapter Twenty-Four

"FOR A TIME there, I felt like we were on the right track, but now nothing feels right about any of this," Julie said when he joined her at the window. Aidan had gone to sleep, and the hour was late. A swollen moon sat high in the sky, illuminating her in soft lunar light.

"I've got this nagging feeling that something horrible is going to happen," she murmured.

He knew his cryptic comment about her eventually disappointing someone hadn't helped. Saying it felt like a foggy dream he could barely remember. Though he seemed to have known who she would disappoint, now he had no clue, so his ominous message remained a mystery.

"Something horrible *is* going to happen according to history," he said softly, referring to Thomas' imminent demise. That in itself could explain her nagging feeling. "Until then, all we can do is continue protecting wee David to the best of our ability."

"Right, and let Thomas die." She white-knuckled the windowsill. "Which seems more and more likely considering he won't just stay here at the castle like he should."

"'Tis not meant to be." He pulled her back against him. They gazed out over the woodland and flickering torchlight of Edinburgh. "If he did, history would not unfold as it should."

"I know." She leaned her head back against his chest. "Gotta say, after all these years watching over time-travelers, I thought I had a grasp on what they dealt with, but I had no clue. I had no idea how hard it could be." She sighed. "Because one way or another, I imagine it was just as difficult for all of them."

"Yet, they got through it." He kissed the top of her head. "They faced what they had to, no matter how fearful. No matter how much they worried about letting others down. And they succeeded."

"You're using my own words on me." She turned in his arms. "Don't think I don't remember."

"Aye, but they were *good* words."

He thought back to the day he'd sought her out not just for advice but the comfort of being with someone who had always been there for him. She was every bit as important as his kin. More so, actually.

"You knew this day was going to come," she had said, strolling through the Salem Stonehenge with him. They were out to enjoy the autumn day and its riot of colors. "You knew you'd become chieftain."

"Aye, but I didnae think 'twould come so soon." He watched her out of the corner of his eye, wishing he could pull her into his arms at last. Wishing she could stay by his side as his wife when he became laird. "Da is still plenty young enough to be chieftain."

"But old enough to want to enjoy a few years with your mom before he's too old," she pointed out. "He and Milly deserve it more than most." Her eyes widened. "You know how much work goes into running a clan, especially one the size of yours." She shook her head. "You're still young, unattached, well-liked, and pretty damn smart, so it makes sense to hand the reins over to you."

"What if I dinnae measure up to da?" He sighed. "What if I let them down?"

"You can't think like that." She stopped and met his eyes, her hair turning to pure fire in the setting sun. "Not only are you amazing with others, but you're the son of Adlin and Milly MacLomain." She perked a brow. "Not to mention you're an arch-wizard." She shook her head again. "How could you even doubt yourself for a second? I certainly don't."

"Because you only see the good in me," he muttered. "You dinnae see my flaws."

"Sure, I do." She quirked the corner of her mouth. "You're stubborn and a little too picky about women, in my opinion."

"Picky about women?" Because none of them are you. But he couldn't say that. "Lasses arenae a priority right now." He shrugged

and moved the conversation along. "And the stubbornness cannae be helped. I'm Scottish." He slanted her an amused look. "Those are my only flaws, then?"

"Yup, and honestly, I'm not so sure I would even call your stubbornness a flaw." She grinned. "Mostly, it's just charming."

"Och, you really do only see the good in me then."

"Maybe, but then you make it easy." She crossed her arms over her chest and looked at him with both compassion and a sternness she rarely displayed. "If Adlin feels confident enough that you're ready to take over, then I do too." She gave him a pointed look. "That means there's no room for fear and insecurity. It's time to serve your clan the way you were always meant to. You face what you have to, no matter how fearful you might be." She shook her head, knowing him all-too-well. "No matter how much you worry about letting others down."

The sun sank more and hit a stone in such a way that for a second, it seemed like her fiery hair connected to it through a long stream of light.

Much like the ley-lines now guiding them.

"Bloody hell," he whispered, returning to the present, absolutely certain he was right. "'Twas your magic even then…struggling to break free."

"I followed what you were thinking about," she murmured, contemplating. "You know I never realized how often we went to that Stonehenge. How many conversations we had there."

"Often and many," he concurred, amazed now that he gave it more thought. "You took me there to explore when I was a child, then coached me through my teenage years at those verra stones."

"I even brought you there when you were an infant," she said softly, fondness and amazement in her eyes. "Come to think of it, that particular stone was the first one I brought you to in order to show you…"

When she trailed off, he finished for her.

"To show me the sun set over the stone that aligns with the summer solstice," he said softly. "And you took me there on the actual solstice."

"Wow," she whispered. "What are we supposed to make of that other than my magic possibly being at work already?"

He thought about it. What other relevance it might have.

"Typically, the solstice is a symbol of new beginnings and ends." He cocked his head in consideration. "Though many cultures believe many things, your magic seems tied in with the Celts. For those from Ireland, the summer solstice was a time to honor Goddess Etain." He narrowed his eyes. "'Twas also a time to banish evil spirits and open up a path towards light and abundance which typically meant a good harvest. But I sense Guardian Witches meant it quite literally."

"They did," she said softly, certainty in her eyes as they met his. "My ancestors harnessed the power of the solstice to banish the Disinherited when they tried to stop Adlin's conception. Essentially they opened up a path of light and a way forward for the MacLomains. A way to exist and do all the good they would do over the centuries." She shook her head. "And I don't think anyone, wizards and mortals alike, knew about it. Not until us right here right now."

"And now the evil spirits, or Disinherited, are no longer banished," he replied. "But have found a way to return."

"Yes." She nodded, a strange look in her eyes, her voice momentarily deadpan. "They were a secret brotherhood. Righteous, entitled men with dark hearts." She blinked several times, snapping out of it, her tone normal again as she put his concern for her at ease. "I'm okay. That was my ancestors speaking through me." She shook her head. "Not the bad guys."

"Grant was absolutely right," she went on. "We're at the beginning of something that won't be easy to banish, but because of us, I think we have access to the light again. We stand half a chance of wiping out what's rising up." Her eyes met his with conviction. "We've got to close off access to the Calanais Stones though. If we don't do that, they'll harness the power of the other sites far too easily, and there will be no stopping them."

"Yet we still dinnae know how to do that," he murmured.

"We will," she said softly, suddenly distressed. "Soon too." Fear flashed in her eyes. "Whatever it is we need to do to close off the Calanais Stones from the Disinherited ties in with the bad feeling I have." She pressed a hand to her chest. "It hurts my heart, Tiernan." Her eyes welled. "There's this heaviness…like unimaginable grief."

"'Twill be all right, lass." He wrapped her up in his arms. "'Tis always all right when MacLomains go up against evil."

She didn't respond, just wrapped her arms around him and held on tight. Eventually, she whispered, "Can we pretend for tonight that everything's normal?" Her eyes returned to his. "That we're simply visiting a medieval castle and getting ready to go to bed like a normal couple?"

Yet another thing he had longed for over the years.

"Aye, lass." He brushed a curl back from her cheek. "I would like nothing more." He offered a crooked grin, determined to put a smile back on her face. "What, precisely, do you mean by normal, though?"

"Anything that doesn't include trying to figure out what's next." She stood on her tip-toes, cupped his cheeks, and brushed her lips across his. "Anything that makes me forget all the bad stuff that might lie ahead."

Of the same mind, knowing full well what she needed, he propped her on the window ledge and came between her thighs. He didn't chant them out of their clothing but kept things as normal as possible. Yet he soon realized normal was nearly impossible when it came to her. When it came to the feel of her lips opening beneath his and the sweet taste of her tongue.

He kept one arm around her to anchor her safely and explored her soft, womanly contours with his free hand while continuing to kiss her. Sometimes lightly, sometimes more passionately, all the while relishing the feel of her. From the curvature of her breasts to the downy softness of the fine hair at the nape of her neck. He ran his hand along her delicate collarbone then down the side of her waist.

As he touched her, she did the same, feeling him as though she'd never felt him before, exploring his chest, arms, and abdominal muscles with eager hands. The more her passion grew, the more impatient she became, wrapping her legs around his waist, tugging at his tunic.

"Patience, lass," he murmured against her lips, thrusting slowly against the material between her legs, teasing. "'Twill come soon enough."

"Yeah, it will," she murmured back. Suddenly, their clothes vanished without being chanted away. Had she done that? She must have. Before he could make sense of it, before he even had a chance to note her eyes weren't quite right again, she grabbed his arse and steered him into her.

Caught by the exquisite sensation, he couldn't pull away even if he wanted to. All he could do was grasp her backside and thrust deep. She cried out and dug her nails into his back, but he barely felt it. All he felt was the mind-blowing sensation of being inside her. The feeling of thrusting, again and again. Drawing closer to what he ultimately craved. What he needed like nothing else.

"Follow me," she gasped. "Follow it back to me."

Assuming she meant release, he did just that, thrusting one last time as she locked up and hit her pinnacle at the same moment as him. Lost in the feel of her milking him, it took a moment to realize she cried softly against his shoulder.

"What is it, lass?" he whispered, sensing those weren't tears of joy. He tilted her chin until her eyes found his. "What's the matter?"

"That's part of the horrible feeling I've got."

"What's part?"

"You," she whispered. Her lower lip wobbled. "You're at the heart of my grief, Tiernan." She shook her head. "Because I can't be certain you follow it back to me."

Chapter Twenty-Five

THE NEXT DAY dawned dreary, a bleak beginning to even bleaker news.

"Is Thomas serious?" She frowned at Tiernan and Aidan. "Tell me he's joking."

"Nay, the wee lad is in the courtyard ready to leave." As upset as they were, Aidan shook his head. "I cannae imagine what Thomas is thinking bringing the king beyond the safety of these walls. Especially when he knows he'll be fighting Balliol."

"I dinnae think he's thinking clearly at all." Tiernan gave them a grim look. "I think one of the Disinherited is at work here."

"But why not finish the wee king here then?" Aidan said. "Why draw this out?"

"Because they need something," Julie murmured, sure of it. "Something they can't get if they simply kill him here." She met Tiernan's eyes. "Remember, there's more to this than Balliol becoming sole king."

She tried not to think about her ominous, possibly prophetic words to Tiernan the night before. Her gut-wrenching sensation that he was at the root of her growing dread. If that weren't bad enough, Adlin had finally made contact with them telepathically, fearing for his son's safety. Though he said it was just a father's natural concern, she knew there was more to it.

"He sensed something was going to happen to you," she'd said to Tiernan as they cuddled in bed. *"I'd bet my life on it."*

Naturally, Tiernan kept assuring her it would be all right, but they both knew something awful loomed.

"My magic's growing by the second, and you know it," she had argued. *"Just look at how I removed our clothing without even chanting!"* She'd frowned at him. *"So you know damn well I'm right. My magic is trying to warn us about something."*

"Or," he had countered softly. *"Prepare us for the inevitable."* He'd shaken his head. *"You know as well as I that your magic is following the path your ancestors have laid for it. That means 'tis leading you in a direction, showing you the way."* He had shrugged a shoulder. *"Is there a warning in that? Verra likely. But we both know 'twas not given so that we would cower in fear and not continue our journey."*

"I hate when you're right," she'd whispered because he was. They were supposed to keep moving forward. They were supposed to follow the light into the darkness. She knew it like she knew nothing else.

So though tempted to now say, "We could use our magic to keep David here," she knew better.

She offered the boy a comforting smile as Aidan and Tiernan conversed with Thomas about travel plans. Unfortunately, David was surrounded by guardsmen so she couldn't get any closer, but when the boy's eyes met hers, she knew her smile was welcome. Though he tried to be brave, bone-deep, he was terrified.

"I swear I felt his emotions," she said into Tiernan's mind later that day as they traveled. *"He senses something off about Thomas too, and he's really scared. Yet he refuses to show it and appear weak. Poor kid. What a life he's been thrust into."* She frowned and sighed, hunkering down against the blustery wind and rain, thankful for Tiernan's warmth at her back. *"No child should be going through this. Especially on such a crappy day."*

"Aye," Tiernan agreed. *"But there is naught we can do about it, but stay close and protect him the best we can."*

Yet Thomas, despite her protecting the king before, kept them at a distance, which only fed into the theory he was possessed.

"I know," she mumbled aloud, noting Aidan's watchful eyes and grim expression. "Why do I get the feeling your cousin is on alert for more than just the enemy?"

"Because he is," Tiernan replied. "He feels as though Chloe is just around every corner. 'Tis a growing unease he cannae shake."

"Unease?" She frowned at him over her shoulder. "That doesn't sound promising."

"Nay, but 'tis hard to know with him if the unease comes from being destined for a lass other than Maeve," he said, "or if 'tis related to something more."

"I'd guess a bit of both." She looked ahead again, taking in the endless woods. "Where do you think we're heading anyway? Where do you think Balliol is?"

"I dinnae know, lass," he said. "He could be anywhere."

"Right," she murmured, thinking about it. "Where does Thomas supposedly die again?"

"Musselburgh."

"Do you anticipate us getting that far today?"

"Aye," he replied. "By nightfall."

She met his eyes again, fresh dread kicking her pulse up a notch. "So today's the day then?"

"Mayhap." Tender strength lit his eyes as he went into chieftain-mode. Something he'd been doing more and more as the day wore on. "'Twill be all right. Things will go as your ancestors have directed, and we will defeat whomever we are meant to defeat."

Though she knew he was right, that he had to be if they hoped to help everyone, she feared it because she knew it would come at a high cost. She dreaded to think what that might be, though.

"You must put that from your mind, lass," he whispered in her ear, reminding her of their shared words. "You face what you have to, no matter how fearful you might be. No matter how much you worry about letting others down." Then he added to it. "You follow your light and do what you must. Do the right thing."

"How will I know what that is?" she whispered back, her dread only growing.

"You'll know." He kissed her cheek softly. "Because you'll do what I would do."

"I don't know if you're the best example." She turned her cheek enough to meet his eyes, her heart in her throat, referring to him breaking the rules at the beginning of their adventure. "You didn't do what you were supposed to do."

"I did exactly what I was supposed to do," he reminded. "I just didn't know it yet." He searched her eyes. "But my gut did, Jules. My verra heart and soul." He put his hand over her heart. "That's what you have to follow when the time comes. Where *this* tells you to go. What *this* tells you to do."

"Okay," she managed dutifully, trying to be strong. "But only because you're pulling your inner chieftain on me, and it's damn effective."

"Good." He offered a small smile. "'Tis helpful when the chieftain's lass listens to him." A twinkle lit his eyes. "'Tis not always a sure thing, as seen with several Brouns of the past."

"I can just imagine." She chuckled, referring to one of the most recent ones. "I bet your mom led your clan as readily as your father if not more so sometimes."

"Aye." He met her chuckle. "She's a strong-minded woman."

"Good thing." She winked at him. "Best to keep you MacLomains in line."

"A few of Thomas' scouts have returned," Aidan commented into their minds, pulling them from their conversation. *"Two that I can tell."* His eyes went to Tiernan. *"Their expressions arenae reassuring."*

"Nay." Tiernan frowned. *"I think 'tis only a matter of time before—"*

When someone roared, "Defend the King," ahead, her blood turned cold.

"Let's go, Cousin!" Tiernan roared. She held on tight when he unsheathed his blade and spurred his horse alongside Aidan.

"Och, 'tis bloody hard to see in all this fog," Aidan said into their minds. *"Where the bloody hell is it coming from all of a sudden?"*

"It's them," Julie murmured, sure of it. *"It's my ancestors at work...or me."* She shook her head. *"I'm not sure. All I know is it's trying to hide David and—"*

"You," Tiernan exclaimed, figuring it out a second before she did, just as men came out of nowhere and attacked. *"They didn't just want the king destroyed but to take you!"*

Something that would have been far more difficult to accomplish back at the castle. Why did they want to take her, though? If anything, she would think they'd want to kill her.

"Sonofabitch," she muttered, whipping a dagger at a warrior who rushed her from the left. Meanwhile, Tiernan ran his sword through a man to their right then spurred the horse on.

"We need to get to David," she exclaimed. "*You* need to, Tiernan."

"I will," he assured, punching another guy that rushed them. "We both will."

Suddenly, everything seemed to go into slow motion as they raced through the fog. It was almost as if she were suspended in time though everything was still chaotic around her. A sense of peace and certainty settled over her. Certainty she knew was born of her magic.

It gave her a sense of direction.

"I can get us to him," she whispered, narrowing in on the fog. More so, the ley-lines that appeared through the fog overhead, lit by sunlight even through the cloud cover. "I'll get us to him."

She looked from her ring to the lines, then closed her eyes and centered herself, tuning out the warriors Tiernan and Aidan fought. Instead, she followed David's fear, his sheer terror, as they were attacked. She followed it until it was a trail of light in her mind that attached to the ley-lines.

"We're coming," she whispered. "And we'll save you no matter what."

She sensed the Claddagh ring igniting the path of light in her mind.

"That way," she exclaimed before light flashed around them.

When she opened her eyes, they appeared mere feet from the king.

"We're here, David!" She and Tiernan leapt off the horse and took up arms in front of the child cowering beside his horse. "Just stay there! We won't let anyone near you!"

Yet they were severely outnumbered with no sign of Aidan.

"I'm calling to him telepathically," Tiernan said into her mind, *"but he's having trouble locating us."*

"I know," she replied, fighting the best she could. *"Pretty sure it's the Disinherited interrupting my magic."*

"Aye." He cut down three warriors at once. *"Just stand guard in front of the wee king. I will fight whatever comes at us."*

Unfortunately, what came at him next was the last person they wanted to see.

"Take the lass," Thomas roared, referring to Julie. His gaze was off, his eyes lecherous as he went at Tiernan. "I will deal with the enemy."

"Bloody hell, I am nae the enemy," Tiernan roared, trying to get through to Thomas, trying to break through his possession to the man beneath. He kept pleading with the regent to see the truth of things as the two went at each other, but it made no difference.

In the meantime, she cushioned David between her and the horse, surprised by how calm the animal was with all the mayhem around it. They must be trained for it in this era.

"Snap out of it, friend," Tiernan roared at Thomas, growing desperate.

It did no good, though.

The regent was too far gone to the evil inside him.

"I havenae any choice," Tiernan said sadly into her mind, his brogue thickening with his emotions. *"My magic isnae working, and I cannae let him near ye and the wee king."*

He would have to end Thomas before the regent ended David.

"Do what you must," she replied gently, trying to offer comfort and strength. *"No matter what others think of you, do what's right, Tiernan. Your country has to come first. That means David has to come first."*

"Aye, lass." His internal voice suddenly sounded far away.

A bizarre wave of panic blew through her.

What the hell? What *was* that?

A split second later, she knew.

It had been a dreadful premonition.

Things seemed to go in slow motion again, except this time, it wasn't her magic igniting. Rather her world was about to come to a screeching halt. Someone got ahold of her and yanked her away from the king. Terrified for David, she kneed the guy, dropping him long enough to turn back.

Yet she had taken one second too long.

Her worst nightmare unfolded before her eyes.

Thomas ran his sword through both Tiernan and the king when Tiernan leapt in front of David. A blink of an eye later, Aidan appeared out of the fog and ended Thomas Randolph in turn.

Chapter Twenty-Six

"OH MY GOD," Julie cried, sheer terror in her wet eyes. She fell to her knees in front of him and the wee king. "Please don't leave me, Tiernan."

He blinked, trying to understand what had happened. One moment he had been fighting Thomas, the next defending the king. Seconds later, he felt the sting of a blade.

Yet when he looked down, there was nothing there.

"Oh, thank God," she whispered over and over, blinking several times, evidently seeing the same thing. "I must've..." She shook her head, tears pouring down her face when David peeked his head around Tiernan. "You're both all right." She kept shaking her head. "It didn't happen. Just like before, it didn't really happen."

Tiernan inspected the king, relieved to see she was right. "You saved us, lass." He embraced her, grinning. "You did it."

"Where are we?" David whispered, his eyes wide as saucers. "And what happened to my horse?"

That's when it occurred to him they weren't in the foggy forest anymore but at the Calanais Stones. Fog still drifted around the standing stones only now the rocks almost appeared ignited by sunlight.

David's white horse, however, was by far the most startling sight to behold as it grazed nearby.

"Tell me I'm seeing things," Julie whispered, chuckling nervously. "Because that horse looks like it's got a damn horn attached to its forehead."

"It does appear that way," Tiernan concurred softly.

It couldn't be what it appeared to be…could it?

Yet it had to be with its slender golden chains.

They approached carefully.

The mystical beastie never moved but chomped the grass as though it didn't have a care in the world. He studied the horn from every angle, even touching it with the horse's permission.

"'Tis indeed a horn," he murmured in awe. His magic flared to life. "And this beastie is indeed verra much a unicorn."

Julie chuckled again and shook her head. "Yeah, right." She winked at David. "Tiernan's being silly."

"I dinnae think so," David murmured, resting his hand against it. "'Tis Scotland's animal." His trembling subsided, and warmth lit his eyes. "'Tis our verra power."

"'Tis many things, lad." Tiernan patted the unicorn affectionately. It continued munching away. By all appearances, it wasn't magical, just plain old hungry. Though Tiernan looked at David, he subliminally pointed out to Julie one of the reasons it might be here now. "In Celtic mythology, it symbolizes innocence and purity." He met her eyes. "Also, healing powers, joy, and even life itself." He shrugged a shoulder. "'Tis also seen as a symbol of masculinity and power."

"What's with the golden chains around it?" she asked.

"The Scottish unicorn is always depicted bound by a golden chain wrapped around its neck and body." He was relieved to find the glittering chain lightweight and delicate, not cumbersome. "Believed to be the strongest of all animals, wild and untamed, the unicorn is only humbled by a virgin maiden. Her purity strikes a chord with its equally pure spirit. Therefore it allows her reins of gold." He shrugged. "'Tis also said the rope symbolizes the power of Scottish kings, entrapment if you will, seeing how they were strong enough to tame even a unicorn."

"Interesting." She spoke within his mind. *"What's with yet another reference to virgins on our journey? Because it seems sort of coincidental, don't you think?"*

"'Tis a wee bit bizarre," he conceded, not convinced it had anything to do with them. Mayhap someone to come? *"Are any of your friend's virgins?"*

"God, no," she replied, then seemed a little unsure. *"Or so I assume…do you think that's what this is about?"*

"Time will tell," he replied. *"Or mayhap it willnae because 'tis really only a coincidence."* He shrugged, yet he got the sudden sense he was onto something. *"Then, there is always the distinct possibility that the purity of the unicorn somehow fulfilled the old requirements of Guardian Witches in all this."* He shook his head. *"So, you did not need to be virginal, to begin with."*

"Do you really think so?"

"'Tis as good a theory as any, aye?"

"It is," she murmured, clearly sensing something. *"Why do I suddenly get the feeling I owe this unicorn a great deal of gratitude?"* She ran her hand along it, sounding convinced. *"Because eliminating my virginal requirements changed the rules."* Her eyes met his. *"That's why I was able to sleep with you and not lose my magic."* A small smile curled her lips. *"Once that happened, the Claddagh ring's magic took over, and we found added power the old fashioned Broun, MacLomain way despite my lack of lineage."*

"Aye," he agreed. *"I believe you have the right o' it, lass."*

Never so grateful, he continued patting the unicorn.

"Do ye think the unicorn helped save us?" David said, pulling them from their internal conversation. His eyes were hopeful, at last showing some of the whimsical joy a bairn his age should feel. "Do ye think it helped save me because it thinks I should be king?"

"Aye, I think Scotland's national animal would have done precisely that." He crouched in front of the boy and met his eyes, quite serious. "Because ye are verra much my king. One who I know loves this country every bit as much as yer ma and da ever did."

"Aye, I do," he confirmed, puffing up a little, saying what he thought he should say. "I only hope I dinnae let my good da down."

"Och, ye couldnae." Tiernan shook his head and rested his hand on the boy's shoulder. "Remember that, King David. Remember that ye are strong, brave, and honorable. Ye will always be such, no matter what happens."

Fresh hope lit his eyes. "Ye really think so?"

"I do," Tiernan confirmed. "Now we best get ye back to yer keepers, aye?"

"Aye." David eyed the stones curiously. "But where are we? Where did everyone go?" His lower lip trembled. "And what happened to Sir Thomas? I was too afraid to look."

Thank God for small favors because if Tiernan knew nothing else, it was that Aidan had definitely ended the regent's life. Something he suspected would weigh heavily on his cousin's shoulders but had to be. It was also something had David seen it, might have made things difficult for Aidan down the line.

"Something that's got to be making life difficult for him right now, Tiernan," Julie said into his mind. *"Especially if others saw him kill the regent."*

"Verra true," he replied. *"But best not to worry about that until we get back and find out what's going on."*

First, he had to prepare David despite how hard it might be. Babying the boy would not do him any favors. Not with what he likely faced when he returned.

After all, Scotland without a regent was not good.

So he told David as gently as he could that Sir Thomas would not be with them anymore. He had lost his life. Therefore, David had to be especially brave now. Yet he should always keep in mind that he wasn't alone. Tiernan and his fellow MacLomains would stand by him during the difficult transition.

Though tears welled, David blinked them away and nodded, sadly used to this sort of news.

"See, ye really are *verra* courageous," Tiernan praised. "I am verra proud to call ye my king."

David stood up a little straighter, gratefulness in his eyes before he looked at the stones again. "Best that I get back then, aye? Best that I return to my warriors."

"Aye." Tiernan squeezed his shoulder gently, nodded once, and stood. "'Tis time to go."

"Do you think it'll be like before?" Julie said into his mind. *"Once we step beyond the stones, we'll end up where we're supposed to be?"*

"We can only hope." He pointed out the stones. *"Because like before, these look newer."*

"So, you think we traveled way back in time again?"

"Quite possibly." He noted the sun. *"And like before, the sun is getting ready to set."*

"It is, isn't it?" She swallowed, her eyes worried as she put a hand to her stomach. *"That feeling of dread's returning, Tiernan."*

"All is well, though," he assured. *"Thomas died as he should, and the wee king remains alive."*

"I know," she whispered aloud. "But something still feels off."

"Let us walk beyond the stones then," he said gently, convinced her magic still suffered the aftereffects of what had happened. Something he shared telepathically. *"You controlled your magic for the first time to get us to David during the attack. Doing such almost feels like shock afterward. 'Twill make things feel verra off."*

"Maybe." She frowned. *"It's not so much a numb feeling of shock, though, but the same exact dread I felt last night. Which makes no sense at the moment."* Her worried eyes met his. *"I shouldn't feel dread, should I?"*

"'Tis hard to know." He tried to sense her magic and mayhap how she felt but was unable to. *"This could verra well be normal when it comes to your particular magic, lass."*

She nodded but didn't appear convinced. They tried to leave the circles only to find they couldn't.

"What's going on?" Her startled eyes met his. *"We've never been unable to leave."*

"Nay." He frowned and lifted his sleeve.

"There's no line on your tattoo," she began but stopped when the sun hit the top of a stone and an orange stream of light cut across his tattoo, pointing in a direction.

So they headed that way but were again stopped by an unseen barrier.

"I see something this time, though," she whispered, squinting through the fog. "I see…"

"Oh, God," she whispered, horrified. Her eyes welled, the color drained from her face, and she shook her head. "No…please no…tell me I'm not seeing that…"

Moments later, he saw it too.

Though still in the circle of stones, they were just beyond where they had been before in battle. The horse had vanished, leaving a clear view of what was left.

He and David lay dead on the ground where they had been killed.

Which meant they weren't actually standing here. At least not in the physical form. Yet thankfully, they could still feel one another.

"No," Julie cried. She pressed her face against his chest when he pulled her into his arms. "Tell me it's some sort of trick. That the Disinherited are behind this."

"I cannae tell you that, lass, and you know it." He stroked her hair in comfort, seeing everything so clearly now. "I think we both know what has happened. What you have to do."

"I don't know jack shit," she whispered into his mind, not wanting to frighten David any more than he already was. She met Tiernan's eyes with defiance. *"Don't tell me you're really dead. That we're dead."*

"You're not dead, lass." He brushed his finger along her cheek tenderly. *"I am."* He cherished her every feature while there was still time. *"You are still alive, Julie."* He looked at David, hoping she understood. *"As is one other of your choosing."*

Choked up with the very grief she had prophesied would come, she put a hand over her mouth and shook her head in denial.

"You face what you have to, no matter how fearful you might be." He cupped her cheek and told her what she needed to hear. Because he already knew what he would do regardless of her decision. *"No matter how much you worry about letting others down. You follow your light and do what you must. Do the right thing."*

"You," Julie cried into his mind. *"You've always been the right thing, Tiernan. From the very beginning."* She kept shaking her head. *"Please don't make me choose between you and him."*

"But you must." His magic flared. His understanding only grew. *"A sacrifice cancels out a sacrifice."*

Seconds later, she realized what he just had.

She saw the truth.

"The Disinherited sacrificed something on a tomb in Ireland." Her eyes drifted to the one here. *"And it took root on that very tomb."* She blinked, seeing what Tiernan saw. The dark magic Adlin and Grant had sensed as it blossomed on the rock and wrapped around the Guardian Witch magic already here. *"What did they sacrifice that had that kind of power, though?"*

The unicorn wasn't eating anymore but stared directly at them.

Just like the Guardian Witches had when surrounded by these very stones.

"The unicorn," she whispered aloud before remembering to speak within the mind. *"As far as I know, unicorns aren't bad, though."* She frowned, confused. *"So how could evil gain headway out of sacrificing one of them?"*

"Because the Disinherited harnessed the power of the act itself," Grant said softly, appearing beside the animal, more solid here. But then here was technically the afterlife. "For there is nothing more evil than sacrificing such a mystical animal, never mind that 'twas done out of vengeance and greed."

"That's so sad," she whispered, wiping away a tear. While he knew she felt for the animal, her tears weren't for it but for what was coming. What she knew she had to do. "Grant...why are you here?"

"You know why he's here, Jules," Tiernan said softly, proud of her. "Because you've already made your decision." He met her eyes. "You can save one of us. The other must be sacrificed." He looked from David back to her. "And you know who that must be. You know who must be saved."

"This isn't fair," she whispered, tears rolling down her cheeks. "This isn't how it's supposed to end."

"But it is." He brushed away her tears and cupped her cheeks. "This is how it was supposed to end from the verra beginning, lass." He searched her eyes, wanting to stay with her as long as possible. Yet they were almost out of time. The sun was setting. "I'll always be with you, Julie. My magic, my heart," he brushed his lips across hers, "my verra soul."

"I just can't," her lower lip wobbled, "this is too damn much."

"You can," he said firmly. "And you will."

"But I'm your protector," she said on a strangled whisper.

"And you have protected me well." He pulled her into his arms one last time. "You got me where I needed to be to help protect my king and country. You've served me well, Guardian Witch."

"Don't call me that," she mumbled against his chest, sobbing softly. "I don't want to be called that anymore."

"Yet 'tis what you are, lass." He tilted her chin until her eyes met his again. "My Guardian Witch." He searched her eyes, hoping she saw, *felt*, how convinced he was of his own words. "You will find me again someday, Julie. In another life. Just like you did this one. Have faith in that. Have faith that we're tied together now in a way we never thought possible." He brushed his lips against hers again. "Let that bring you comfort."

Before she could answer, he kissed her one last time with everything he felt then pulled away. He looked from the setting sun to her. "'Tis time, lass." Bloody hell, this was hard. "'Tis time for you to do what you must."

"What is happening?" David asked, clearly not understanding. Protected, mayhap, by Julie's magic itself.

Her tortured eyes lingered on Tiernan before she dragged them away and offered David a warm, albeit teary smile. "It's time to go back and continue ruling your country." She held out her hand. "I'll take you there if you like."

David nodded and took her hand before he looked at Tiernan, more astute than he anticipated for one so young. "Ye arenae coming with us, are ye?"

"I'm afraid not, lad." He rested a hand on David's shoulder. "But I know ye will remain courageous and rule well, aye?"

David pulled his shoulders back a wee bit. "Aye."

"The light comes," Grant said softly. "'Tis nearly time, Julie." His sad eyes met Tiernan's, and he nodded. "'Tis time, lad."

Moments later, the sun hit the same spot on the stone it had when the Guardian Witch's power was at its greatest. When the ring had been created. A long stream of orange light shot from the stone to Julie and in turn, David.

"It looks just like the stream of light I saw when I held you at the Salem Stonehenge when you were an infant." Tears continued running down her cheeks as her eyes met his one last time. "I love you, Tiernan. I'll always…"

Sadly, he never heard the rest of what she said before she and David vanished into the light.

Chapter Twenty-Seven

GRIEF-STRICKEN, JULIE allowed Aidan to embrace her as Tiernan's body was taken away.

He was gone. *Truly* gone. She could feel it bone-deep. Soul-deep.

"He's really dead," she whispered, crying. "I thought…maybe…"

She couldn't get the rest out. Her grief was too consuming. Deep down, she had hoped by the grace of God, Tiernan would miraculously be alive like David had been when they returned, but no. The horse was gone, David was alive, and Tiernan lay dead at her feet.

Now she understood why he'd said the prophetic words 'she would disappoint someone' back at Edinburgh Castle while under the influence of magic. Because she had. Herself. What kind of protector was she that she couldn't bring him back with her? That she couldn't keep him safe? Alive?

She also now understood her own prophetic words about fearing he couldn't follow 'it' back to her. *It* had been the stream of solstice light that had returned her and David. The light Tiernan couldn't follow.

"I know 'tis hard, lass," Aidan murmured, having as much trouble as her coming to grips with Tiernan being gone. "'Tis impossible to believe…to accept."

As it turned out, the fog had been so thick that no one saw who killed Thomas Randolph. They assumed it was the enemy, which made things considerably easier for Aidan. Not that he seemed all that thrilled. As Tiernan had surmised, he struggled with what he'd done, despite the fact that it had to happen.

"We must return to MacLomain Castle," he eventually murmured. The same deep sadness she felt reflected in his eyes. But then he had lost a brother, hadn't he? "We must...tell his kin."

"Oh, God," she whispered and pulled back. "How am I supposed to do that?" She wiped away a tear, beyond heartbroken. "How am I supposed to tell Adlin and Milly their son's gone? That, in the end, I couldn't protect him?"

"You protected what mattered most to him, lass," he said gently. "You protected David, his country, and most especially, yourself."

"But I was supposed to protect him!"

"Protecting you *is* protecting him," he replied. "You mattered more to him than life itself, and you know that."

She did know that, but it didn't make this any easier. Not at all. She was all twisted up inside. Unable to come to grips with him being gone. She could barely swallow, let alone breathe. Caught in a heartbreaking state of limbo. Strangely numb while still saturated in grief. This, she would have told Tiernan, was shock. Because if all her emotions were getting through right now, she wouldn't be standing but curled up in a ball on the ground lost in despair.

"Lord, this hurts," she whispered, her chest tight. "But not nearly as bad as it's going to once reality truly sets in."

There would be no more waiting anxiously for Tiernan to appear in New Hampshire. No more of that heart-soaring feeling she'd had when he finally showed up. She'd had no idea just how much a part of her he had become. Though it had only been a year and a half since she first met him, it felt like a lifetime of memories. He was her best friend. The love of her life. How would she go on without him?

"I know it hurts," Aidan said softly. "But you're not alone. Tiernan's kin is your kin, Julie. Never forget that."

She swallowed hard and watched as David's retinue made their way back in the direction of Edinburgh Castle. With the chaos of men trying to come to the king's aid, she'd only managed to give David a brief hug goodbye, assuring him he would see her again soon.

"Balliol's troops have fallen back and shouldnae be a problem for a while yet," Aidan said. "I will return with you and—"

"No." She rested her hand on his forearm, met his eyes, and shook her head. "It's your turn to watch over David, Aidan." A strange sensation washed over her that she now recognized as magic. Magic that told her she and Tiernan had accomplished what they'd set out to do. "Chloe will be coming soon. She'll help you." She closed her eyes, sensing something before she opened them to his again. "The Calanais Stones are a safe place for MacLomain wizards now…a bridge built for what will likely happen next."

When he frowned in curiosity, she went on. "The rock you and Chloe were trying to find each other around led somewhere…" She kept exploring the sensation until she understood. "The Ring of Brodgar Stonehenge."

"Should I go there then?" he said. "Is that where your friend will be?"

"Likely…eventually," she confirmed. "You have to follow David first, though." She squeezed his forearm, making sure his eyes stayed with hers. "You have to protect him, Aidan. The rest will take care of itself."

His brows furrowed. "You're sure, then?"

"Positive."

Evidently, he trusted her because he didn't question her further only nodded in understanding and embraced her. "Let my kin know I'm well, aye? That my magic feels stronger now." He pulled back and met her eyes. "And know that 'twill be all right…they willnae blame you for anything, Julie. They love you."

She offered him a wobbly smile, praying he was right. "Stay safe, Aidan, and thank you for coming along. For helping us out."

"I wouldnae have been anywhere else." He hid his grief well, but she still saw it in his eyes. "Tiernan was my best friend too."

She nodded, blinking back fresh tears before she looked to the sky and ley-lines. Not surprisingly, the one leading to MacLomain Castle was brighter than all the rest. So she closed her eyes, envisioned the castle, then opened them again. She choked back a sob when she appeared at the very spot they had stood when she first saw the castle days before.

Not surprisingly, Adlin and Milly stood beside the oak as if waiting for her.

You can do this, Jules, Tiernan would have said. *Face what you have to, no matter how fearful you might be. No matter how much you worry about letting others down."*

"I miss you so much," she whispered.

She tried to draw on his strength but only felt a vast emptiness. It was incomparable. Impossible to describe. To go from finally feeling the kind of love and connection she shared with Tiernan to this terrifying chasm of nothing.

Walk, she told herself, but she couldn't seem to put one foot in front of the other to go to his parents. She couldn't close the distance and confirm that the fear in their eyes was justified.

But she had to.

For him.

For them.

"I owe you this much," she whispered, finally finding the strength to go to them. To push the terrible tale past her lips and watch them embrace each other in grief.

"We were right," Milly whispered, sobbing. "We felt him go."

Julie stood there, awash in her own grief, not sure what to say or do. How to comfort them.

"Come here, sweetheart," Milly said softly, finally leaving Adlin to embrace Julie. "And you don't have to comfort us. Not when your pain is as deep as ours, if not deeper."

Grateful, she held on to Milly then embraced Adlin next only to feel a strange sensation wash over her. This time the sensation wasn't quite her magic. Adlin pulled back with a confused look before light blue magic sputtered to life in his eyes.

"Grant was there when my son passed on, aye?" he murmured, his gaze widening in sudden disbelief. "And a...*unicorn?*"

"Yes." She looked at him in confusion. "What just happened, Adlin? What was that between us?"

Because whatever it was most certainly sparked when they touched.

"My son...I think." His eyes narrowed. "Through you...I think."

"You *think?*" Milly said, incredulous. "You don't *know?*"

"'Tis fluctuating, lass," he murmured in explanation, eyeing Julie over as he tried to figure something out. "Where is the blade? Where is the sword our Viking ancestors gave Tiernan?" He tilted his head in question. "Did you give it to Aidan?"

"No." She shook her head, thinking about it. "The last time I saw it, Tiernan had it." She frowned. "Come to think of it, it wasn't by his body when I returned either."

"So 'tis safe to say it wasnae stolen off his body whilst ye were in between." Adlin's brogue thickened with emotion. "That he indeed had it at the Stones."

She nodded, more hopeful by the moment simply because he seemed to be. "Yes, but I don't recall it doing anything special." She shook her head. "No lightning on the blade or anything."

"Well, no, of course not when ye were amongst the Celtic gods in that circle." He shook his head, clearly lost in his own mind as he paced and rambled on, wearing his white robes and holding his cane in the blink of an eye. "'Twas a sword made by the Norse gods yet allowed within a circle of Celts..." His eyes rounded, having clearly seen it all in her mind. "With a sacrificed unicorn no less!"

He kept shaking his head and pacing. "Yet 'twas all there in one place with the magic of a Guardian Witch and an arch-wizard and a Claddagh ring and—"

"Adlin," Milly exclaimed. She seemed to sense something because she stopped him and met his eyes. "What is it?" Her gaze narrowed. "What's that pressing feeling I'm having?"

"Pressing feeling," Julie whispered. "Like we're running out of time..."

"Och, that's it," Adlin exclaimed, his eyes rounding on Julie. "I needed to connect with Grant!" He shook his head. "Or at least all he could share through ye and yer magic, lass."

"And," Milly prompted when he seemed quite pleased he had realized that.

"And what?"

"And what's this damn pressing feeling, husband!"

"Och, right." His eyes shot to the setting sun then returned to Julie. "We need to return to your stones."

"The Calanais Stonehenge?" She shook her head. "Why what's going on, Adlin?" Hopeful when she shouldn't be, her heart leapt in her throat. "Is it Tiernan? Is he—"

"We need to get to your stones," he kept saying. "That is all I know."

"The Stonehenge, then?"

"Aye," Adlin confirmed. "The Stonehenge." His gaze flew to the sun again. "Before the sun gets much lower or 'twill be too late." Grave, he shook his head. "'Twill be far too late."

She nodded and looked to the ley-lines, locking onto the brightest one without giving it too much thought.

"I'll do my best to bring you along, but I'm still fairly new at this," she murmured, closing her eyes, envisioning the Stonehenge. Then she envisioned Tiernan's gorgeous blue eyes. How they looked when they last met hers in the circle, then when they connected at the door in New Hampshire when he came for her, then further back still.

She remembered them meeting hers at the Stonehenge at Mystery Hill when she knew she'd fallen in love, then further back when he was a teenager making doe-eyes at her. Then further back to when he was a little boy, helping her collect sticks for kindling. Then when he was a toddler playing in the autumn leaves all the way back to...

Julie opened her eyes and gasped.

She wasn't at the Calanais Stonehenge but at the Stonehenge in New Hampshire. She even stood in the same spot in front of the stone aligned with the summer solstice. Most importantly, though, she was doing what she had been doing that day.

She held Tiernan as an infant.

"Oh my God," she whispered.

Her eyes met his at the precise moment the sun hit the top of the stone.

A ray of light cut across and hit them both as his eyes sparked with magic. She tried to keep her gaze with his, but the light became too bright. She closed her eyes to a flash of lightning only to find him vanished when she opened them again.

Instead, something was coming from the ray of orange light cutting over the stone.

Better yet, *someone.*

Chapter Twenty-Eight

NOTHING WAS MORE heart-breaking than watching Julie vanish into the stream of orange light leading her back to life.

Until that is, it led her back around to him.

Or so it seemed.

Yet she wasn't moving, was she?

Even so, he saw her.

She was right there waiting for him…holding something.

Curious, he drifted toward her though he knew he should stay. But something about going to her felt like returning to himself. So he walked and walked, wondering what she was gazing at so lovingly until he heard the crackle of lightning over his blade.

She looked up, then squinted, closed her eyes as if blinded, then opened them again.

Close, closer, closer still, then she was right there.

Right in front of him.

"Julie," he whispered, confused. "What are you doing here?"

"Tiernan," she whispered back, tears spilling over as she stared at him. "Is that really you?"

"'Tis." He touched her cheek. Something he never thought he would do again. She was real. Here. "Why are you back? Why are you not with David?"

"Oh my God, I can *feel* you," she sobbed and embraced him. "You're actually *here*."

"Aye, right where you left me," he murmured, holding her just as tightly.

That's when he realized he wasn't where she had left him. Not at all.

Rather he was at the Salem Stonehenge in New Hampshire.

"How did I get here?" he said, confused. "I dinnae ken."

Moments later, the summer day faded, and the weather changed entirely.

It was winter again.

"We're back." She met his eyes. "Really back." She glanced over his shoulder. "And the sword's gone."

She was right. It had vanished.

"You best get in out of the cold then, aye?" came Grant's voice moments before his ghost appeared out of nowhere. "I think you'll find things just as you left them."

"Just as we left them?" Julie frowned at him. "Are you sure?"

"Aye, thanks to the Viking sword." He seemed quite pleased despite his ethereal form catching on a gust of snowy wind before stabilizing. "'Tis as I'd hoped. Our ancestor's magic is allowing time to pass as we need it to, which this time wasn't all that much different than how it normally would have."

"That's welcome news indeed." Tiernan chanted fur cloaks onto him and Julie without a second thought. "So time passed in Scotland, but not here?"

"From what I can tell," Grant confirmed. "Mayhap a few hours or so here." He tapped his temple and winked at them. "Long enough for a certain lass to dream about my great-grandson at a certain Stonehenge."

Julie nodded, clearly glad to hear that. "With any luck, Aidan will be waiting for Chloe when she arrives."

Grant nodded, more pleased still.

"What about my sword, though?" Tiernan frowned between them. "And can someone bloody well tell me what's going on already?"

So Julie did as they headed for the house only for Grant to point out that they might want to head somewhere else first. Going back to the colonial wasn't the only way in out of the cold.

"I can just as well explain what happened from my end at MacLomain Castle." Grant's eyes met Tiernan's. "Your parents would verra much like to see you, lad."

"But what if I can't get back here like before?" Julie asked.

"I dinnae expect that you getting here will be a problem now," Grant said. "Not since you were willing to sacrifice Tiernan for King David. A noble, selfless act that sealed the Calanais Stones off from the Disinherited, therefore, allowing you to travel through time more freely. At least from that location." He appeared truly impressed. "You've made far greater progress in all this than you realize, lass. Just take a moment and feel it…understand it."

Julie stopped and looked from Grant to the ley-lines. Then she glanced back in the direction of the Stonehenge before she looked toward the house.

More specifically, the old oak tree out front.

"I feel it," she whispered and met Tiernan's eyes. "Do you?"

First, he felt it within her mind then all around them. An unbreakable connection to the ley-lines he had not felt before. One of those lines led not only to the Salem Stonehenge but directly to the tree.

"There's still darkness here, though," Julie murmured. Her eyes turned back in the direction of the stones. "It's faint, but there."

"Aye, but 'tis not as strong as it was before," Grant murmured. "Is it?"

"Nay," Tiernan replied, sensing more. "The Disinherited are weakened and werenae able to track what just transpired betwixt us there." He looked at Julie. "Though we have time and can now return without issue, 'tis all right to stay here." He took her hand. "Just as long as we're together."

It was still hard to believe he had been brought back to life and looked forward to hearing why as much as Julie clearly did. When she peered at the house, he knew she sensed what he did. Her friends slept soundly and were safe for now.

"No, it's okay." She squeezed his hand. "Let's go back to the castle. Your parents want to see you."

"You sense them now, aye?" he said softly, sure of it. "Ma and da?"

"I do," she murmured. "While I'd started to a little earlier, it's been really strong since I hugged your father."

"Aye." Grant grinned. "'Twas a much-needed connection too. The final piece in bringing you two back together the way the good Lord intended."

"He did intend such," Tiernan murmured. "All the gods did."

"Let's go home, Tiernan," she said softly. "Your family's waiting for you."

He liked that she called it home and hoped she meant it.

In fact, he would see her mean it. Right here. Right now. Too many moments had already gone by. Too much life left behind. But there was also life ahead, and he wanted it to be with her.

So rather than wait another moment, he fell to a knee, be damned the snowy ground.

"What are you doing?" she whispered, her eyes wide.

"You know what I'm doing." He held her hand, fully aware that her ring's gem glowed continuously now with the color of their eyes. "I have wanted to marry ye for as long as I can remember, lass. Ye and only ye. Ye're my closest friend and the love of my life." He kissed the back of her hand, keeping his gaze with hers despite the swirling snow. "Nothing stands betwixt us anymore, Jules. So give me what I long for. What I feel like I've longed for since the beginning of time." He looked at her with his heart in his eyes. "Marry me. Become my wife."

Tears welled, and she nodded, clearly trying to speak but unable to find her voice. She cleared her throat and tried again, this time having luck though her voice wobbled. "Of course, I'll marry—"

That's all she got out before he pulled her into his arms and kissed her long and hard. Eventually, he murmured into her mind, *I never thought I'd do this again. At least not in this life.*

"Me neither," she murmured and deepened the kiss even more.

He had no idea how long they stood like that, simply relishing the sensation of being in each other's arms again before she whispered into his mind, *"I think we have a new audience."*

Only then did he realize she had shifted them back to the fourteenth century, and his castle. His parents were standing nearby, amused as they watched them fondly. Not surprisingly, they had already been filled in telepathically by Grant about everything, including Tiernan and Julie's engagement.

"I'm sorry," Julie started to say as she pulled away, embarrassed that she'd been caught in the act, but his mother cut her off.

"What for?" Ma grinned and looked between them before smiling at his father. Naturally, she referred to Tiernan and Julie's passionate kiss when her gaze returned to Julie. "As far as I'm concerned, that's a great way to time-travel, my new daughter."

Happy embraces were shared all around.

"Congratulations to you both!" Da beamed at them before he winked, as eager for grandchildren as ma. "Now 'twill only be a matter of time before your wee ones arrive." Before anyone could respond, his father embraced Tiernan again, holding on a little longer this time. "'Tis bloody good to have you home, Son. You gave us a good fright, but made us verra proud." He looked between Tiernan and Julie. "You both did. Verra much so."

"'Twas something else," Tiernan replied, happier to see them than he let on. He might not have been gone long, but that didn't dispel the fact he thought he'd never see them again. Any of them, for that matter.

Soon after, they were welcomed home by a clan who still didn't know magic existed but were as content as they ever were.

"Welcome home, Cousin." Ethyn clapped Tiernan on the shoulder. "I look forward to hearing about your adventure."

"Are Cray and Marek still here?" Tiernan asked. Thanks to his magic being intact again, he knew the answer before Ethyn had a chance to respond. "They've returned to MacLeod Castle then." He narrowed his eyes, sensing even more. "You all dreamt of the stones in Ireland, aye? An unknown lass beyond the fog? Mayhap even evil?"

"Aye, and it rattled our dragon kin something fierce," Ethyn confirmed. "That's why they returned home so swiftly. To be amongst fellow dragons to try and figure things out until they heard from you."

"Yet you dinnae seem all that rattled by your dream," Tiernan observed.

"Nay." Anticipation lit Ethyn's eyes. "'Twas quite the opposite for me." He cocked his head in consideration. "I felt honored to be there...favored."

Tiernan and Julie glanced at each other, having no idea what to make of that.

"'Twill be all right, Cousin," Ethyn assured, grinning as they crossed the drawbridge. "'Twas a good experience." He eyed Tiernan, noting the change. "So, you can sense your fellow wizards again, aye?"

"Aye," he confirmed, understanding. "Yet you cannae sense me, aye?"

"Nay."

"I think it takes time," Julie said. "The more Stonehenges we get under our control, the better."

"Which means better understanding what happened when we nearly lost wee David and did lose Tiernan," Grant said, appearing out of nowhere as he was want to do. He met Tiernan's eyes. "Which means understanding how you ended up here when you should be long gone."

Chapter Twenty-Nine

"SO THE UNICORN did it?" She would have been more incredulous if she hadn't seen the mystical animal with her own two eyes "I assumed it was a ghost like you, Grant? A symbol of the sacrifice?"

They sat in the MacLomain's great hall, enjoying a much-needed drink. It had been one hell of a journey emotionally, from losing Tiernan to knowing with certainty she would be spending the rest of her life with him.

"The unicorn was a symbol of the sacrifice made," Grant conceded. "But 'twas also much more. 'Twas the protector of Scotland." A knowing look lit his eyes. "And as you both already figured out helped a wee bit when it came to purity." He winked at them. "Or lack thereof." He shrugged a shoulder. "But above all, as I said, 'twas ultimately protecting Scotland."

When Adlin arched a brow at him that he may want to elaborate, Grant went on, his ethereal form catching on the faces on the mantle here and there, making them seem alive. Truth told, they were on occasion. MacLomain ancestors listened intently from the beyond via those many visages. She homed in on one friendly face she knew thanks to her magic. Grant's wife Sheila waited patiently for him to return to the afterlife.

"Whilst everything came together as it should to create the magic needed to resurrect wee David, including the beastie itself with the power of healing," Grant looked at Tiernan and Julie, "'twas the length to which you two would go to see through your pledge, not just to this country but to each other, that warmed the unicorn's heart for lack of a better explanation. Add in the Guardian Witch protective connection you made with Tiernan so long ago, 'twas no wonder the beastie helped you."

"Not to mention the unicorn had a wee bit o' revenge on those who slayed him," Adlin added. "For bringing you two back together will only aid in the fight against this unknown brotherhood. A brotherhood which no doubt has ill intentions toward the beastie's beloved Scotland."

"Verra true," Grant agreed.

"So the Disinherited *were* trying to psyche us out when they possessed me and said you'd already failed to see through your pledge," she said to Tiernan. "Because you definitely saw it through despite breaking the rules in the beginning."

"Aye." He squeezed her hand, certainty in his eyes. "And they willnae be possessing you again." He shook his head. "Not anymore."

"No, not me," she agreed, as certain as him. Yet she remained worried about her friends. "But maybe others."

"Dinnae forget your friends have the power of the Claddagh ring behind them from the start," he reminded. "That in itself may protect them."

"I hope so," she murmured, perplexed. "I'm curious about something, though."

When everyone looked at her curiously, she went on.

"As far as I know, there are five more Claddagh rings to be worn by five of my friends," she said. "Yet, I've only met five men with MacLomain blood that seem to be part of all this." She cocked her head. "So who's the sixth guy? Who haven't I met yet?"

"We wondered the same thing, lass," Adlin said. "Because you are now with the fifth lad."

"So what gives?" She looked back and forth between Adlin and Grant. "Who is my fifth friend meant for?"

"We dinnae know," Grant said. "It may be a cousin more removed than immediate kin."

"Has that ever happened before with a Broun?"

"Nay," Adlin replied. His eyes twinkled as he looked at her and Tiernan. "But then just look at you two. So times are changing indeed."

"Indeed," Grant echoed.

She eyed the ghostly wizard, her mind back on what he had said about the unicorn. "So what's this about warming the unicorn's heart, Grant? What does that mean exactly? Is it something that will benefit my friends too? Help them out along the way?"

"I think by helping you, it *has* helped them," he replied. "Not to say it might not make another appearance or two before all is said and done." His gaze flickered between her and Tiernan. "As to precisely what it means to warm a unicorn's heart? It means your love was so true it spoke to the mystical beastie on a level beyond that of a Guardian Witch and her protector." His gaze went to her ring. "Even beyond the true love connection of the Claddagh ring."

Julie and Tiernan glanced at each other, not doubting their love was strong enough. Yet, could such a thing really happen? Had a unicorn come to their rescue in the end? She liked to think so. In fact, the more she thought about it, the truer it became. They looked at Grant, knowing it was his magic that allowed them to see clearly. To feel the truth. After all, not only was he a powerful wizard but a direct connection to the afterlife and in turn, the unicorn.

She also knew without question that her ancestors' magic had very much been present in that stream of sunlight that followed her. It had not only guided her where she needed to go but guided her true love back to her.

"What about the need for a sacrifice, though?" Julie said softly, sure she was right about this. "A sacrifice that will be needed at every Stonehenge in the end."

"Sacrifices come in many forms, lass," Tiernan said softly, sensing something. "'Tis not always a life."

"Nay, 'tis not," Adlin concurred, his eyes wise as he too sensed the truth of it. "Something must always be forfeited to be gained in this." His gaze went to the faces on the mantle. "What that is only time will tell."

"Time," Grant murmured. "Yet another telling factor in all this."

"It is, isn't it?" Julie said softly. "Sunset."

"Aye," Grant replied. "When combined with Guardian Witch magic, 'tis the source of power in what lay ahead for the others."

"'Tis also the ticking clock," Tiernan murmured, understanding. His eyes met hers. "We've started building the bridge, but 'twill be up to the others to keep building."

"Until they reach the end." She narrowed her eyes. "I haven't a clue what that is, though."

"You will in time," Adlin said, his gaze a little haunted. "We all will."

"So five Claddagh ring's, five friends, four MacLomains that I know of," she murmured, mulling it all over. "Plus, the power of the solstice at sunset…each at a consecutive Stonehenge." She narrowed her eyes in contemplation. "Three Stonehenges left in Scotland now, maybe one in New Hampshire." She shook her head and looked at everyone. "If my magic's right in how this is supposed to go, we're still down one Stonehenge…unless we include the stones in Ireland."

"Which I suspect we do considering the dream you've all had about it," Adlin said softly. The look in his eyes told her he had, in fact, saved Tiernan and Julie from their dream.

"'Twas a hell of a dream." Tiernan eyed his father. "And one where the stones didnae appear as they had been but instead like my mysterious tattoo."

"Yet another unsolved mystery in all this," Adlin murmured. "Though I suspect I've figured out why we witnessed the Stone of Destiny at the beginning. Our beloved coronation stone."

"Aye," Grant said, of the same mind it seemed. "A connection to all kings of Scotland and as I mentioned before magical in its own right."

"Much like the unicorn," Adlin went on, "the Stone of Scone, or Stone of Destiny, is a symbol of this country and as such, could only ever lend Scotland protection." He looked at Julie. "I believe it helped guide you to the Calanais Stones because you supported the true king, the *rightful* king, and meant to protect him."

"Well, I'm grateful." She cocked her head. "Do you think it will help again?"

"'Tis verra likely," Grant murmured, gazing into the distance as though seeing something no one else could. "'Tis important in all this. Important in all the changes that lie ahead for we MacLomains and Scotland itself. What those changes are will reveal themselves eventually." His eyes met Adlin's. "Until then, we must continue on the journey laid before us and keep a vigilant eye on wee David."

Adlin nodded in agreement.

"Do you think 'twill be like this every time?" Ethyn asked, having been caught up on everything and clearly wondering what lay ahead for him and his fellow wizards. "Do you think those of us with MacLomain blood will end up killing a regent possessed by the Disinherited?"

"'Tis impossible to know, but I dinnae sense it will be that cut and dry." Grant sighed, likely thinking about Aidan and the guilt he undoubtedly carried. "The fact remains, however, to keep David on his destined path, regents must die as they will."

"Who's the next one?" Julie asked. "When and where is he supposed to die?"

"His name is Donald, Earl of Mar," Adlin said. "He'll be elected by an assembly of the magnates of Scotland at Perth, on the second of August in our Lord's year, thirteen thirty-two."

"And die but ten days later," Grant added gravely. "Battling Balliol and his Disinherited at the Battle of Dupplin Moor."

"That's awful." She frowned yet knew things were happening the way they were meant to. They were right on track for now, and her and Tiernan's magic was intact.

"What about my sword?" Tiernan asked. "'Tis clear it played a big part in all this." His brows swept up. "Should I assume it found its way to Aidan."

"Aye," Grant confirmed. "But I will double-check on that once I leave."

"You know we never did figure out why Thomas heard my accent as local," she remarked.

"'Twas always your magic protecting you," Grant said. "'Twas trying to keep the Disinherited possessing Thomas from figuring out the truth about you."

"Though it already had when it possessed me," she countered. "No matter how brief." She shrugged. "So, what's the point of me continuing to sound like that to him?"

"Magic like yours is much like your immune system fighting off an infection," Adlin explained. "'Twill keep trying to fight off anything that means to harm you even if 'tis too late."

Milly perked a brow at him. "Interesting analogy, husband."

He grinned at her. "I thought so."

"So, what's next?" Ethyn asked. "Should I join Aidan?"

"Soon but not yet," Grant murmured, clearly sensing something. "Eventually, though, for I fear a dragon will not be far behind."

191

"Cray." Julie narrowed her eyes, listening to her magic. "Following Maeve."

"Aye, Maeve," Grant confirmed. "Or so we assume."

When everyone looked at him in question, he merely shrugged. "As Julie and Tiernan just discovered, 'tis not always easy to know who's who when dealing with dark magic." His eyes went to Adlin. "Especially magic determined to manipulate us before we even had a chance to begin."

Manipulate not *end.*

Begin not *be born.*

"They wanted it, didn't they?" she said softly, figuring out what Grant and Adlin already knew. "The Disinherited didn't want to end Adlin before he was conceived in another life, but be part of the process itself. Take what they felt they had a right to for whatever reason."

"Aye," Adlin said darkly, his gaze momentarily haunted again. "They wanted the Druidess…and then they wanted the power to do with Scotland what they would. Much like Balliol's nobles want their Scottish land and power over this country even though they turned traitor."

He shook his head, then continued. "Both groups consist of greedy, lecherous souls, so 'tis no wonder they're aligned in this though 'tis yet to be discovered precisely how. My guess is by possession as that seems to be the brotherhood's way." His eyes met Julie's. "Now, they want the Brouns and the extra power they bring with them. But they will have to go through a MacLomain to do that." He shook his head. "And my bloodline willnae allow it any more than the magic of the Claddagh ring will."

She nodded, feeling his certainty. His very strength.

"So, what's next?" She looked at everyone. "Probably best that I get back to New Hampshire, I'd think."

"Oh, I think you still have time, lass," Adlin replied. His haunted expression was swiftly replaced by a smile and a twinkle in his eyes.

"Most definitely," Milly kicked in, meeting his smile.

"I couldnae agree more." Tiernan swept Julie up into his arms, his brogue thickening with his emotions, his joy at finally having her where she was meant to be. "I think 'tis far past time ye finally see my chambers, *our* chambers, *then* we will marry and get back to the future."

She perked a brow and chuckled. "Aren't we supposed to marry before you whisk me away to our chambers?"

"Aye, mayhap if we had gone about things in the proper order." He met her chuckle. "But 'tis too late for that, and I grow impatient."

There was no need to ask why because she felt the same. Not just impatient to make love again, but to spend every waking moment together. To finally not just be friends, but much more. So he carried her to their chambers, and at last, showed her precisely what to expect in his bed every night.

And every morning.

Hell, every day into the unforeseeable future.

They hadn't defeated the enemy yet, but they were one step closer. Tiernan had seen through his pledge to kin and country, Balliol's Disinherited had been weakened, and they would weaken them even more until they ended them once and for all.

Until then, it was time to bask in what had been denied them for so long...

Love that had been theirs from the moment their eyes first met.

Coming Soon

Torn between the lass he still loves and the Broun destined for him, Aidan sets out to protect wee King David from Balliol and his disinherited only to end up at The Ring of Brodgar Stonehenge, then soon after America's Stonehenge in the future. Having been unknowingly summoned by Chloe and her ring, his arrival there does not go unnoticed. An ancient brotherhood is watching.

Pursued by darkness that can be anywhere at any time, he returns to protect David with Chloe in tow, determined to do right by his kin and country. Yet his level nature is soon tested when his overly inquisitive Broun takes them down a path that tests his resolve and challenges his lonely heart. Will he remain devoted to his long lost love? Or will defeating evil mean embracing someone new? Find out in *A Scot's Devotion* (The MacLomain Series, End of an Era, Book 2). Now available for pre-order.

Stonehenge & Stone of Destiny

America's Stonehenge (Mystery Hill)
Salem, New Hampshire
United States

While the first mention of the site was in 1907 and no pre-Columbian artifacts have been found, some still believe that the site is over 4000 years old. On the equinoxes and solstices, people flock to the area to watch the sun rise and fall over the huge chunks of granite, deciding for themselves whether or not they're standing amid relics of prehistory.

Calanais Standing Stones
Callanish, Isle of Lewis
The Outer Hebrides
Scotland

Erected between 2900 and 2600 BC, the Callandish (or Calanais) Stones are an arrangement of standing stones placed in a cruciform pattern with a central stone circle or tomb. They're on a low ridge above the waters of Loch Roag with the hills of Great Bernera behind them.

Ring of Brodgar
The Orkneys
Scotland

Erected between 2500 BC and 2000 BC, the Ring of Brodgar stands on a small isthmus between the Lochs of Stenness and Harray.

Machrie Moor Stone Circles
Machrie
Isle of Aaran
Scotland

Erected around 2030 BC, the Machrie Moor Stone Circles is a collective name for six circles formed of granite boulders, while others are built of tall red sandstone pillars.

Clava Cairns Stones
The Highlands
Scotland

Around 4000 years old, the Clava Cairns Stones are a cemetery complex of passage graves; ring cairns, kerb cairns, and standing stones.

Stone of Scone (Stone of Destiny)

According to one Celtic legend, the stone was once the pillow upon which the patriarch Jacob rested at Bethel when he beheld the visions of angels. From the Holy Land, it purportedly traveled to Egypt, Sicily, and Spain and reached Ireland about 700 BC to be set upon the hill of Tara, where the ancient kings of Ireland were crowned. Then it was taken by the Celtic Scots who invaded and occupied Scotland. Around 840 AC, it was taken by Kenneth MacAlpin to the village of Scone.

Stone of Destiny
Modern Day Scone Abbey (Monastery of Scone)

Founded between 1114 and 1122, Scone Abbey was a house of Augustinian canons located in Scone, Perthshire, Scotland. Originally named Scone Priory, its status was increased in 1163/64 to Scone Abbey.

Author's Note- the abbey my characters visited in this book no longer exists but in July 2007, Archaeologists pinpointed the location using Ground Penetrating Radar technology. The Abbey's structure was revealed to be larger than had been imagined. The exact location was what is now a garden area in front of Scone Palace and Moot Hill.

Stone of Destiny
Coronation Chair

The Coronation Chair was made by order of King Edward I to enclose the famous Stone of Scone, which he brought from Scotland to England in 1296, where he placed it in the care of the Abbot of Westminster.

-A Scot's Pledge-

Previous Releases

~The MacLomain Series- Early Years~

Highland Defiance- Book One
Highland Persuasion- Book Two
Highland Mystic- Book Three

~The MacLomain Series~

The King's Druidess- Prelude
Fate's Monolith- Book One
Destiny's Denial- Book Two
Sylvan Mist- Book Three

~The MacLomain Series- Next Generation~

Mark of the Highlander- Book One
Vow of the Highlander- Book Two
Wrath of the Highlander- Book Three
Faith of the Highlander- Book Four
Plight of the Highlander- Book Five

~The MacLomain Series- Viking Ancestors~

Viking King- Book One
Viking Claim- Book Two
Viking Heart- Book Three

~The MacLomain Series- Later Years~

Quest of a Scottish Warrior- Book One
Yule's Fallen Angel- Spin-off Novella
Honor of a Scottish Warrior- Book Two
Oath of a Scottish Warrior- Book Three

-A Scot's Pledge-

Passion of a Scottish Warrior- Book Four

~The MacLomain Series- Viking Ancestors' Kin~

Rise of a Viking- Book One
Vengeance of a Viking- Book Two
A Viking Holiday- Spin-off Novella
Soul of a Viking- Book Three
Fury of a Viking- Book Four
Her Wounded Dragon- Spin-off Novella
Pride of a Viking- Book Five

~The MacLomain Series: A New Beginning~

Sworn to a Highland Laird- Book One
Taken by a Highland Laird- Book Two
Promised to a Highland Laird- Book Three
Avenged by a Highland Laird- Book Four

~Pirates of Britannia World~

The Seafaring Rogue
The MacLomain Series: A New Beginning Spin-off
The Sea Hellion
Sequel to The Seafaring Rogue

~Viking Ancestors: Rise of the Dragon~

Viking King's Vendetta- Book One
Viking's Valor- Book Two
Viking's Intent- Book Three
Viking's Ransom- Book Four
Viking's Conquest- Book Five
Viking's Crusade- Book Six

~The MacLomain Series: End of an Era~

A Scot's Pledge- Book One
A Scot's Devotion- Book Two

-A Scot's Pledge-

A Scot's Resolve- Book Three
A Scot's Favor- Book Four
A Scot's Retribution- Book Five

~Calum's Curse Series~

The Victorian Lure- Book One
The Georgian Embrace- Book Two
The Tudor Revival- Book Three

~Forsaken Brethren Series~

Darkest Memory- Book One
Heart of Vesuvius- Book Two

~Holiday Tales~

Yule's Fallen Angel
+ Bonus Novelette, Christmas Miracle

-A Scot's Pledge-

About the Author

Sky Purington is the bestselling author of over fifty novels and novellas. A New Englander born and bred who recently moved to Virginia, Purington married her hero, has an amazing son who inspires her daily and two ultra-lovable husky shepherd mixes. Passionate for variety, Sky's vivid imagination spans several romance genres including historical, time travel, paranormal, and fantasy. Expect steamy stories teeming with protective alpha heroes and strong-minded heroines.

Purington loves to hear from readers and can be contacted at Sky@SkyPurington.com. Interested in keeping up with Sky's latest news and releases? Visit Sky's website, www.SkyPurington.com, join her quarterly newsletter, or sign up for personalized text message alerts. Simply text 'skypurington' (no quotes, one word, all lowercase) to 74121 or visit Sky's Sign-up Page. Texts will ONLY be sent when there is a new book release. Readers can easily opt out at any time.

Love social networking? Find Sky on Facebook, Instagram, Twitter, and Goodreads.

Want a few more options? "Follow" Sky Purington on Amazon to receive New Release Kindle Updates and "Follow" Sky on BookBub to be notified of amazing upcoming deals.

-A Scot's Pledge-